MARCO
IMPOSSIBLE

MARCO
IMPOSSIBLE

HANNAH MOSKOWITZ

FISH

Roaring Brook Press

New York

SQUARE FISH

An imprint of Macmillan Publishing Group, LLC
175 Fifth Avenue, New York, NY 10010
mackids.com

Our books may be purchased in bulk for promotional, educational, or business use. Please contact your local bookseller or the Macmillan Corporate and Premium Sales Department at (800) 221-7945 ext. 5442 or by e-mail at MacmillanSpecialMarkets@macmillan.com.

Library of Congress Cataloging-in-Publication Data
Moskowitz, Hannah.
    Marco impossible / Hannah Moskowitz.
        p. cm.
    Summary: "Two best friends and junior high students attempt to break into the high school prom so that one of them can confess his love for the adorable bass player of the prom band"—Provided by publisher.
    ISBN 978-1-250-14392-1 (paperback)   ISBN 978-1-59643-860-6 (ebook)
[1. Best friends—Fiction. 2. Friendship—Fiction. 3. Family life—Fiction. 4. Gays—Fiction. 5. Jews—United States—Fiction. 6. Mystery and detective stories.] 1. Title.
    PZ7.M84947Mar 2013
    [Fic]—dc23

                                                                        2012021602

Originally published in the United States by Roaring Brook Press
First Square Fish edition, 2018
Square Fish logo designed by Filomena Tuosto

10 9 8 7 6 5 4 3 2 1

AR: 3.9 / LEXILE: 660L

To the Barrie School of Silver Spring, MD
Never grow up.

BLUE SNOW CONES
AND A KARATE MAN

Our last day of middle school was supposed to be amazing, but instead Marco and I are standing at the sinks in the gray boys' bathroom trying to wash half a snow cone out of my hair.

"And we were all excited when they said there were snow cones, too," Marco says. He's scrubbing my forehead with a paper towel. "It's always like that when they bring stuff to school. It's like you've never heard of that thing before, ever. Remember when the cafeteria had limeade that one time? And everyone freaked out completely? Running around all hyped up on limeade."

That was two months ago, April 9th. I don't even have

to check our case file to know that. Limeade Day is still a legend around here. Snow Cone Day was supposed to be, too. It's this big celebration for the last day of school.

I think the universe has tapped into how completely I do not want to celebrate the last day of school.

"That hurts," I say.

He stops rubbing. "Sorry. Here." He hands me the paper towel. I sponge my forehead for a while, but the color isn't going anywhere.

"You should embrace it," Marco says. "Blue hair."

"I don't want blue hair."

"You look like a rock star." He's gone from sounding sympathetic to jealous in less than a second. That's pretty much the most Marco thing in the world.

I say, "You have enough rock stars in your life."

"If only." He leans against the sink, all dramatic. He isn't even pretending to help me rinse my hair out anymore. "If only, if only, if only, Stephen."

I dunk my head under the faucet. When I come up for air, he's watching me in the mirror, his face completely earnest. It's like I said. Marco can change his entire face in the amount of time it takes me to blink. It's like I never know exactly who I'm going to be talking to.

He says, in a voice to match his face, "That was really cool of you, you know?"

"Trust me, I know." I put up with a lot for this kid.

He says, "Getting in the way like that."

Yeah. I took a hit for Marco. What else is new? "Eh. I was already there. It's nothing."

Then his expression breaks, and he gets sarcastic and smiley and jams his tongue into his cheek. "Stephen, you're my faaaaaavorite," he says, in this voice that's probably supposed to make him sound silly but really just makes him sound like he did when he was six. He messes up my hair with both hands, then he laughs at his blue palms.

I decide that he's worth getting a snow cone thrown at me. I'm not always sure.

But it's not like I had any other choice this time. Luke and Chris said that if Marco didn't kiss me, they'd throw a snow cone at us. Marco didn't kiss me. They threw a snow cone at us. Except Marco's a way smaller target than I am, and I guess maybe I was in front of him a little, so most of it hit me. Anyway, it's pretty much the most straightforward thing that's ever happened to me in my whole life.

Except, I guess nothing is straightforward when Marco's involved.

And Marco's my best friend, and when you have a best friend like Marco, he is always, always, involved.

He drums on the lockers on the way to homeroom. Any other day we'd be accosted by some hall monitor for being out after the bell, even though my hair and his stained shirt should count as a perfectly good excuse. But it's the last day of school. These halls are a totally lawless place right now. Some seventh grader runs past us spraying a bottle of Silly String. It streaks behind him like a flag.

A seventh grader has Silly String, and Marco and I, eighth graders—almost ninth graders, now—are just going to homeroom like upstanding citizens or something. Marco isn't looking at me, but I can tell he's thinking the same thing I am: *We should be doing something so much cooler than this right now.*

Marco and I are criminal masterminds. We solve crimes and plan heists. We've apprehended more cellphone thieves, and returned more lost puppies, and sneaked in and borrowed more gym uniforms from the office when we've forgotten ours than most thirteen-year-olds could ever dream of. Just because we're usually on the side of law enforcement doesn't mean we should be shuffling around like sheep on the last day of school, right?

Honestly, this school owes us. Look at that fluorescent light bulb that always flickers in time, perfectly, to the words of "Hey Jude." Who do you think discovered that? And who do you think breaks into the janitor's office and steals all the light bulbs every time they are about to fix it?

Marco, yeah. But I mean...I was there. I'm always there.

He jerks his head toward the front door at the end of the hallway. "Jailbreak?"

"It's raining." It seems like it's raining all the time lately.

He looks outside and sighs. "Yeah."

"Wouldn't be any fun."

"This is terrible. Worst day ever, Stevey. Worst day of my whole life."

I should be used to him saying this kind of stuff. Marco is really dramatic, but, I mean, seriously? I'm the one walking around looking like someone spilled toilet cleaner on me.

"There's cookies in homeroom," I say. I hope this is true. It's a rumor Sasha told me. I don't think schools know any other ways to celebrate things than to feed us.

"Yeah. This is what we have to live for, Stephen. Cookies in homeroom."

Mr. Takeda gives us this long look when we come through the door, but he holds out the tray of cookies without saying anything. There's only one chocolate chip left, so Marco grabs it and hands it to me like he thinks someone's going to snatch it away if he doesn't. "Thanks," I say.

Marco nods all short and confident. His secret agent nod.

Mr. Takeda is still looking at my hair. Everyone's giggling at us a little, but someone makes a noise like a sick sheep over in the corner. Like the world's happiest, evilest sick sheep. I don't even have to look to know it's Luke.

Last day of school, I remind myself, over and over. If the snow cones had worked out, there would have been two good things about middle school ending. Now there's one, and I'll latch on to it. Last day of middle school means the beginning of three months without Luke.

And it means this is Marco's last day of Luke forever, because Marco isn't going to high school with us.

I still can't believe it. *Clinton Preparatory Academy.* It sounds like a school for dogs. And Marco, for some reason, is actually excited about going.

Marco glares at Luke for half a second on the way to his desk, then turns his attention, just like always, to a different boy at the edge of the class. Benji gives him a smile and a brief wave. Marco lights up.

I bite into my cookie and sink into my seat next to him.

These didn't used to be our desks, but I bribed Daniel Rivera with boxes of leftover Girl Scout cookies—I have three sisters, I could repave my driveway with Girl Scout cookies—until he switched with me. Marco gave me a hard time about it at first, but he gave in when he realized that the seat next to my new one has a great view of the back of Benji's head. Besides, it's not like it's big news that I want to sit next to Sasha.

"We were talking about our summer vacation plans," Mr. Takeda says. "Miss McGuire, continue where you left off, please."

Sasha tugs a piece of hair by her ear. I really like Sasha's hair. It's curly and really dark red, like the inside of a cherry. "Just that my parents think that the chances we're going to find real fossils are pretty small, but I've been doing some outside reading, and I think that if we go to some of the places that haven't been checked in a while..."

I am trying to listen to Sasha.

But Marco won't stop pulling on my arm.

"What?" I whisper.

He points his pen toward Mr. Takeda's desk. I immediately see what he's all scrunched up about. There's an action figure, some kind of three-inch-tall martial artist, perched on top of Mr. Takeda's keyboard. There's a rolled-up piece of paper shoved under its arm.

"Wasn't there yesterday," Marco whispers. It's his job to notice these things. Marco is the eyes and ears of our operation.

We haven't done a simple reconnaissance case in a while. To be honest, we haven't done many cases lately.

Marco knows I need to start small again, I think. After our last case.

Aimee raises her hand and tells Mr. Takeda that she's going to Paris and will also be playing a lot of paint ball. Now that Sasha's done talking, I have no reason not to concentrate on the karate man. I can pretend there's nothing else important in the whole world. I hardly even feel my sticky hair anymore.

Marco digs a sheet of paper out of his backpack and scrawls me a note: *Please confirm that the action figure is, in fact, a new item of interest.* Our usual notes to each other aren't this formal, but this one will end up pasted into the case notebook, so it's important it be professional.

I root through my backpack. I can tell Marco is not impressed by how long it takes me to find the notebook.

But I get it eventually, of course. Documentation is my job. I handle the notebook and I take pictures. But it's not as if I can whip out my camera right now, not while Aimee's still teaching the class how to say *protective gear* in French.

I find the homeroom section in my notebook and read through my notes. I don't have anything on the state of Mr. Takeda's desk besides a quick *Note: desk messy* from way back in October. I can't tell Marco that. He'll kill me.

I would have remembered if the action figure were there before. And Marco would have, definitely. *New,* I write. *Confirmed.*

Sasha leans over my shoulder and whispers, "I can't believe you guys are still doing this." She must have just been chewing mint gum, because her breath feels cold in my ear.

I don't know why we still do it. Probably because neither one of us wants to be the one to suggest we stop. My older sister and I used to have these really expansive made-up worlds, and we kept it going for so long, and as soon as she hinted we might be too old it was all over. And this is how Marco and I started off. We hardly knew each other, and then one of the fish in our first grade classroom went missing and we jumped on the case. It's just something to do, but it's just something that's ours.

Anyway, Sasha doesn't sound judgmental, even though she's definitely trying to. She sounds intrigued. She wants to be a journalist, and she can never decide if we're giving investigative writing a bad name or if we're living the dream while she's still stuck in real life.

Mysteries are exciting. This one is starting small, but you never know what one clue will uncover. The mystery of Ms. Lagerman's hamster in fifth grade started out with Peepers looking a little bloated one morning. It ended with eleven hamster babies. Marco got to keep one because he was the one who diagnosed her with The Pregnant. He offered the baby to me, but I thought my sister would eat it.

He nods toward my notebook, so I turn back to it and begin copying down the details of the incident as we know them so far. Desk. Karate man, tilted about forty degrees. I write forty-three because it sounds more technical.

I don't think anyone else in the class has a clue what's going on. Even Sasha doesn't know what we're writing about exactly, and she should really stop trying to sound hardcore and be thankful that Marco and I are keeping a close watch on this school. Without us, no one ever would have figured out that it was the chicken fingers that sent forty kids home puking before they poisoned another batch. Without us, everyone would still be wondering who stole all the dodge balls out of the crate by the playground.

"This school's going to fall apart without us," Marco always says.

I write, *Need to get a closer look,* meaning I think we should stall by Mr. Takeda's desk for a few extra seconds on our way out, but Marco reads this, and then thrusts his hand right up in the air.

Mr. Takeda waits for Aimee to finish talking, then raises his eyebrows at Marco. "Yes, Mr. Kimura?"

Marco says, "Would it be a major interruption to the class if Stephen and I ran a criminal investigation in the background of this discussion? Considering this isn't a real class and that this isn't a real day of school, and that technically speaking it probably isn't an actual criminal investigation. Likely vandalism or property theft. Nevertheless, this is a matter of national concern and importance, and you could be prosecuted for obstruction of justice. If need be."

The guy has no shame. It's like someone removed his shame gland.

I think he's probably just trying to show off, though. He has this habit of playing up everything about him whenever Benji's around, even the parts of him that aren't particularly impressive, which I think is weird, but hey, I support Marco. It's what I do. Even when he's embarrassing. Even when he's a jerk.

"And what exactly will you be investigating?" Mr. Takeda says.

"There's a karate man on your desk."

Mr. Takeda looks at it and frowns a little. Then he crosses over to his desk and picks it up.

Marco groans. "Now we can't dust for prints, sir."

Mr. Takeda takes the piece of paper out from under the karate man's arm. He unrolls it.

Marco says, "No offense, sir, but this is really a job better left to professionals. Here." He gets out of his desk and goes up to the front of the room. "Stephen, come on."

I follow him.

"Boys," Mr. Takeda says, but not like he really cares. He's had Marco in his homeroom for three years. He knows to pick his battles, I guess.

Marco peers over Mr. Takeda's elbow. "It has *X*s over

its eyes, Stephen," he says. "Like when Wile E. Coyote dies in *Looney Tunes*."

I write this down. "I need a picture of that."

"Okay, later. I'm still conducting a primary visual investigation." Marco doesn't know how to share. He's an only child, at least until next week. "He has a scroll or something."

"What's it say?" Benji says.

Marco's head snaps up like it's on a string. He looks at Benji and bites his lip. Then he looks down at the karate man and then back up at Benji, everything around him entirely forgotten.

"Marco," I say.

He looks at me and nods a little, and he's back to reality in time to see Mr. Takeda unroll the scroll. But he barely gets a glimpse of it before Mr. Takeda folds it back up and puts it into his pocket.

"Back to your seats," he says.

Sasha says, "Come on, what did it say? Marco, you saw it."

"I don't know," he says. "It looked like Japanese or something."

Luke mumbles, "You look like Japanese or something."

I turn to him and say, "Hey," but Marco doesn't say anything, so I drop it.

Tabitha and Lauren, who are practically identical but not even related, sit on their desks to try to see what Marco's doing and go "What does it *say*?" at the same time.

Marco recites the only Japanese sentence he knows, which means *I don't speak Japanese.* His dad didn't want him to learn to speak it—I don't know why—but he taught him how to say that, at least.

Except I'm the only one who knows what it means, and that's only because I've heard Marco say it a million times. The whole rest of the class is staring at him, waiting for him to translate. He groans hard. "I don't know what it means. I speak Italian. Not Japanese." He's half-Italian, half-Japanese. Italian first name, Japanese last name.

I say, "Mr. Takeda, do you have any idea who might have left you this karate man? Do you have a secret admirer? Is it your birthday?" I check the notebook. "No, it's not your birthday."

"Back to your seats, boys." But he doesn't seem mad. Just tired.

I look at Marco, silently asking him if we should give

in, and he shrugs and nods so we go back and sit down. In this quiet voice, Benji goes, "Welcome back, Marco."

This moment means so ridiculously much to Marco, I can't even explain.

Meanwhile, Sasha's still rolling her eyes at us. Pretending like she didn't care as much as everybody else what that scroll says. Not that it would matter, because I have to pay attention to everything Benji says to Marco, because Marco will make me confirm everything later. *He smiled, right? He said my name all intense, right?*

Out of all the entries in our notebook, Benji's is the longest, because Marco added little bits of commentary to all his bullet points. Every one of my bullet points.

BENJAMIN JAMES CONNELLY

- birthday: 3/9/97 **(EXACTLY two and a half months before my birthday!)**
- two older brothers: Nathan and Mark **(WHICH SOUNDS LIKE MARCO)**
- plays bass in Nathan's band, THE FLOOR IS LAVA **(I love them.)**
- born just outside of London **(and his accent is perfect)**
- goes back to England every summer for soccer camp **(He plays midfield. Why isn't that already in**

the notebook, Stephen? God. MIDFIELD. He plays midfield.)

- stays in England for the whole summer (I don't want to talk about it. I love him.)
- makes Marco act like a little girl (bite me)

Mr. Takeda says, "Mr. Connelly, would you like to tell us your plans?"

But instead Benji says, "Please tell us what the scroll says, sir. We can't concentrate," and I swear he makes that accent even heavier, which makes him sound all young and innocent, which I guess is the point.

Mr. Takeda says, "I can't really be sure, considering the terrible quality of the translation. Not to mention the penmanship. It's not important, but if anyone knows anything about this, come see me after class, okay? No one's in trouble."

"I was the first one in here," Tabitha says. "And it was already on your desk. I saw it."

I say, "It wasn't here yesterday. It would have been in my report." I hold it up. Luke snickers. Shut up, Luke.

"Thank you, Miss Baker, Mr. Katz," Mr. Takeda says to us.

"It wasn't me," Marco says. "I don't know Japanese."

Mr. Takeda shushes him a little and puts his hand on Marco's desk. It's this really gentle touch, like he's patting Marco's shoulder or the top of his head instead. But he isn't.

"I don't," Marco says. "It wasn't me."

"Looks kinda suspicious to me," Troy mumbles from the back of the class.

Marco turns around. "It wasn't *me*. Why would I do something with a karate guy? I don't even *know* karate."

Sasha lights up. "I know karate! Oh. But I didn't do it."

"Thank you, Miss McGuire. Mr. Kimura."

Sasha and Marco both slump down a little. Mr. Takeda is the only one of our teachers who calls us miss and mister. I think he does it to make us feel old, but somehow it makes us feel way, way younger.

He claps his hands together. "We have ten minutes until assembly. Who hasn't told us their summer plans?"

"Benji hasn't," Marco says, but Katherine starts talking instead, so Marco rolls his eyes and picks his pen up. *HATE CRIME?* he writes in big letters.

I glance at Mr. Takeda. He's doing a really good job at acting calm.

Maybe I write. I don't know. Marco thinks everything is a hate crime, always. There's been this really gross rash of them at the high school lately, and he's waiting for them to hit our school, I guess.

Katherine finishes, and Mr. Takeda gives her a smile and says, "Mr. Connelly, I believe it's your turn."

Benji says, "Not really anything out of the ordinary, sir. Going back to London early Sunday morning."

Marco startles and fumbles with the pen. I pick it up and put it back in his hand. He nods a little, staring at Benji.

Mr. Takeda says, "You won't be at graduation?" We have this graduation ceremony on Sunday afternoon. Our teachers are all acting like it's a big deal. My mom tears up whenever I mention it. It's this whole thing. But, honestly, it's probably going to be really boring, if it's anything like my sister Julia's was. It's just a bunch of teachers giving speeches.

"Afraid not, sir," Benji says. "Flight leaves brutally early Sunday morning."

That's not enough time Marco writes, taking up almost the whole page. Marco writes in huge letters when he's excited. It's why he's not allowed to write the case reports.

Enough time for what?

"Mr. Katz, if you *please*," Mr. Takeda says. I crumple the note up, fast, and he exhales. "Thank you. Don't let me catch you again."

Like there aren't three hours left of school, or something. But I'm perfectly content to shut up and stay out of trouble for the rest of the day—my hair is still blue, okay?—but Marco pulls me over to his desk when homeroom is over. I make a really halfhearted attempt to get away, but he's intense about getting this job done. His attention barely even wavers when Benji walks by and smiles at him. He's serious.

Mr. Takeda says, "I guess you two need a picture." I shouldn't be surprised. Mr. Takeda adores Marco. He's the one who nominated Marco for his big award.

"If that's okay," I say.

Marco nods hard. "We're going to have the perpetrator brought to justice."

Mr. Takeda gives us a tired smile. "It's nothing to worry about. He picks up his thermos and sighs. "I need coffee."

I snap a picture, and Marco sticks out his hand to Mr. Takeda. "Don't worry. Detective work is our life." He doesn't leave until he gets that handshake.

But as we walk out and head toward assembly, Marco's shoulders slump and he sticks his hands in his pockets. He doesn't look like an investigator, just like my exhausted, lovesick best friend. "Benji is my life." He sighs. "And he's *leaving.*"

PORTRAIT OF MARCO AS AN EVIL DICTATOR

Marco isn't just hardcore about detective work and Benji, but about his entire life. He won this big award for being both a really good athlete and a really good student. It's called the Harrison award, after this kid Johann Harrison. My brother Brian went to school with Johann, and he says that, two years after getting the award named after him, Johann broke his ankle trying to run a half marathon during a hurricane, so I have my doubts that he was really all that smart, but whatever.

So Marco gets a plaque up by the principal's office, but the big thing is that he has to go onstage to accept this award while they talk about how great he is, and the whole time this huge version of his school picture is going to be hanging behind him, because our projector got smashed so they can't project it, which also means that instead of a slideshow of our favorite memories we have to all hold up these massive poster-board pictures of ourselves faking smiles in the cafeteria and on field trips through the whole ceremony. Graduation is going to be weird.

Lately Marco's been obsessed with what will happen to the huge picture after graduation is over. When we find our seats at the assembly, he's going on about this again. "Do you think they're going to give it to me?" he says. "Do they think I want it? Do they expect me to put it on display? At my *house*? Like there's even going to be room for pictures of me anymore."

Oh. So we've transitioned smoothly right into his other favorite topic. I sit down and tilt my head back and pretend I'm somewhere else.

"No room for anything of mine," he says. "So maybe I should make sure that I get the picture. I'll make copies of it and put it all over the house. It's the only chance I have that my parents won't forget I'm alive."

"Who's alive?" Benji says politely, settling himself down on Marco's other side.

Marco immediately gets all quiet and scuffs his shoes on the ground and mumbles, "Lots of people." He meets Benji's eyes and gives him a small smile.

If Marco doesn't think Benji knows he likes him, he's as stupid as Johann Harrison.

"He's doing the baby rant again," I tell Benji.

Benji says, "Oh, Marco, you're going to love her. I've wanted a younger sibling forever."

On a normal day I would say, "You can have one of mine!" but today I don't, since I never really mean it, and because Marco would just use it as more evidence that nobody really wants siblings.

Benji really doesn't help my case by saying, "Much better than older siblings, anyway. My brothers are dreadful."

Marco says, "See? The new creature is just going to grow up and tell everyone I'm dreadful."

Benji chuckles and nudges his shoulder against Marco's. He has to squish himself down a little to do it.

Marco beams. Behind us, some seventh grader kicks me in the back with one foot and Marco in the back with the other. Marco winces, and we both almost fall out of our chairs.

Last day of school. Last day of school.

Benji already turned around to talk to Blair Cowry, the blond girl who looks weirdly like my sister, and he doesn't see us get kicked. And before I can do anything, Dr. Slade steps up to the podium and everyone gets quiet. Marco reaches a hand back and dusts off his shirt. If the kid does anything else, I'll spit on him. But he doesn't.

"You okay?" Marco whispers to me.

"Fine. You?"

He doesn't say anything. He's biting down on his lip, though, and I think maybe that kid actually hurt him.

Dr. Slade goes on about how he hopes we've all had a wonderful year full of joy and wonder and the magic of learning and then talks about our graduation ceremony and how we're expected to dress and what time we have to be there and what time we *really* have to be there, and Benji turns back to us and frowns. "What happened?" he whispers to Marco. He touches his shirt.

Marco doesn't look at him. "Nothing. It's fine." His fingers are all tensed up, and he's using them like talons to pick at the sleeves of his jacket. "You can keep talking to Blair," he says. God, Marco. He gets so unsubtley angsty when Benji talks to girls. Benji looks at me, confused, and I shrug. I can't get between the two of them ever, in any capacity, or Marco will kill me.

And seriously, how could Benji not have at least some idea of what's going on? Marco doesn't broadcast that he's gay—he came out last year, the same week our basketball team was in the finals, so nobody was paying attention at all—but it's not at all a secret because *subtle* is not exactly the kid's middle name, and anyone important has known he's gay since he was like five, and he's really, really not subtle when it comes to Benji.

Dr. Slade gets to the part of his spiel about all the awards they're giving out, how Hadley Klane is an awesome artist and Tessa Marin got perfect grades and Marco is a great example of everything they have been trying to do with us, and how they wish they could figure out how to instill their kind of verve or whatever into all of us, and he hopes we'll listen really hard to their speeches so we can learn what makes them so dedicated. Dr. Slade is fine, but the more he talks, the more it sounds like he wants to tie all of them down and dissect them.

"Future Clinton Preparatory president," I mumble.

Marco doesn't look up. "Get over it."

Dr. Slade says, "We're sure they'll provide us with tools and information we can use to nurture many more Marcos and Tessas and Hadleys in the future."

"Many more Marcos," Benji says, with a small laugh,

like he's saying a tongue twister, but Marco's distracted by Luke mumbling something a few seats up. Sasha told me that Luke really wanted this award, which I think is kind of ridiculous, because seriously, who *really wants* an award that makes you have to stand up in front of everyone? Luke keeps coming really close to winning all these awards and not getting them. He thought he was going to be MVP of our lacrosse team and then lost out to some seventh grader. I said we should put that in our notebook. Marco told me to shut up. I don't know.

But this award, unlike the MVP, means the school prints out a seven-foot-tall picture of you, a punishment that just became way more relevant because our gym teacher yanks some cord and bam, a sheet falls off the wall and there are Hadley's and Tess's and Marco's heads eight times actual size, looming over us like UFOs.

Before this, I didn't remember what Marco's school picture looked like, but I knew it must not have been that awful because I wouldn't have forgotten the whining and Italian cursing and enthusiastic questioning of God that the picture would have inspired. So I guess it must just be the size of this poster that makes Marco look both five years old and completely intimidating all at the same time.

Marco sinks down so low in his seat that he almost disappears. More than a few people are laughing, most of them kind of sympathetically. But I know when Marco tells this story later—and he will, a zillion, zillion times— everyone's going to be shrieking and rolling on the floor and poking him with pitchforks. Pitchforks that are on fire.

"It's fine," I say to him.

"I look like a dictator. Like a *dictator*."

I say, "Benji, tell him he looks good," but when I turn to Benji, he's talking to Blair again, and Marco slides out of his chair and right down onto the floor.

MARCO'S LOCKER

Marco's still moping while we're walking out of assembly, and he finally says, "I can't believe he's leaving before graduation."

It takes me a minute to figure out he's talking about Benji, which is stupid, because Marco's always talking about Benji.

I shrug my backpack back over my shoulder. "You knew he was leaving."

"I thought I had until Sunday. Until a month ago, I thought I had all of high school…" Because he only decided about the private school thing a month ago. All of a sudden.

"To do what?" I say.

Marco doesn't say anything for a minute, then he pulls me out of the flow of people and into a nook by some lockers. "I'm going to tell him."

And I must be the stupidest person in the world, because for some reason I immediately think *I should tell Sasha* like this is some kind of call-and-response song like we do in music class with our hippie teacher.

"No," I say. "No, you are not."

"Yes," Marco says. "It's time. I'm ready." He takes a deep breath. "I think."

"You think."

Marco breathes out for a really long time. "I've been in love with him for, God, what? Three years now?"

"Sounds right."

"I just…can't go this whole summer without knowing if he's…where I am. Or whatever. At least I'll know."

"So ask him." I say this like it's nothing, but I'm totally freaked out on his behalf. Because I can't imagine trying to tell Sasha. There's no way. Either she'll die without ever knowing that I like her, or there's going to have to be some kind of biblical flood, and we're the last ones on earth, and I can act like I'm only kissing her because I have to.

Marco's talking, but I'm thinking about kissing Sasha, so he can wait for a minute, okay?

He snaps his fingers in my face. "Hey."

God, Marco.

"I can't just ask him," he says.

"Why not?"

Marco groans. "Look, he obviously knows that I like him. I'm not exactly James Bond in front of him. He'd have to be blind not to know."

"So maybe he's not into guys."

"But he flirts with me!"

I don't know. Does he? "Maybe he's just being nice."

"That's why I have to find out. And I have to show him that I'm not just…hung up on him because maybe he likes guys." It's true. Marco's been crazy about Benji since the first time he saw him. Ms. Hoole stood in the front of the room and said, "This is Benji. He just moved here from London," and all of a sudden I was sitting next to a big puddle of Marco. The fact that Benji has never had a girlfriend is either a great sign or a really mean coincidence.

"Tell him tomorrow," I say.

"I *can't*. I need time. I was going to plan something. Something big. I have to *show* him."

Marco's enthusiasm for everyday life can get really, really exhausting, and that's nothing compared to when he's on a mission. I'm tired already.

But also intrigued, because that's what Marco does.

I say, "What were you going to do? Serenade him or something?"

"Or something. Yeah."

"So now you just have to do something before Sunday."

Marco nods. Hard. "You'll help me think of something, right? You'll—"

"—be your sidekick. Yeah."

I guess it should make me mad that I'm always Marco's sidekick. That it's always his big idea and his problem and his victory and I'm just on the sidelines, cheering him on.

And that sometimes he's a jerk to me even though I'm a really, really good sidekick.

I guess it makes me mad sometimes.

But there's nothing I can do to change it, so I try not to think about it. I have enough experience with my humongous family to know that roles hardly ever do.

And when they do, someone gets hurt. So it's fine. And the truth is sometimes I actually really like being the right-hand man.

He nods at me and we get back into the crowd to head over to our lockers. And then we get there, and Marco's locker is smashed in. His stuff is all over the floor.

Whoa.

He freezes a few steps away from the locker and stares at it. His face looks as if he just realized he's in the wrong hallway. He doesn't look mad or upset. Just unsettled and uncomfortable, and a little like he's about to laugh at a mistake he made.

The lockers on either side of his are both fine.

Someone must have done it while we were in assembly, I guess.

There are a few people lingering around the locker who got here before us. They're whispering, and they stop when they see Marco.

"Tabitha went to grab Dr. Slade," Lauren says. "He'll probably be here soon. Did you do it?"

"Of course not."

"Oh," she says, quietly. "I'm sure it was just an accident."

"Yeah."

"Are you okay?"

Marco nods. "Of course, yeah. Stephen, take a picture."

I look at him for a second, but he's not giving me

anything. I clear my throat and say, "Okay." I take a picture, then I take out my notebook and write some stuff down.

I don't know what it is that makes it feel so threatening, but it feels almost like someone smashed Marco.

At least he doesn't seem too bothered.

Marco says, "Guys, can you move? I need to get my books." Once his path is clear, he pries the locker open without looking up.

He doesn't need any books. It's the last day of school.

Anyway, they're all on the floor.

I say, "Seriously, you okay?"

"I'm fine. It's stupid." He tugs out his backpack. It's slit all the way down. "Awesome."

I lean against the locker next to Marco's and flip through my notebook. I'm trying to figure out how long it's been since Marco found that note in his backpack that he balled up and threw away without letting me see it. A few weeks ago, maybe? But he did tell me that whoever wrote it had horrible handwriting. Shaky handwriting.

"Think it's connected to the karate man?" I ask. The least I can do is make him feel like he's the one putting the pieces together.

I see Benji talking to a girl a few feet away. He glances up at Marco's locker.

"What? No." Marco says. He doesn't see Benji.

"Then what about that note in your locker?"

"It's just a locker, Stephen, whatever."

"You're the one who had me take a picture." But I'm being gentle. I swear. "You think there's a case in this?"

"I don't care." He turns around and grabs my arm. "Benji's looking at us. Why am I touching you when Benji's looking at me? He'll think I like you." He lets go of me and shakes his hand off.

"Ew."

One time I thought Marco liked me. For about six hours. Then he told me that my overbite was weird and just because he liked guys didn't mean he liked all guys, hello, was I interested in Daisy Jonesman, yeeeah, that's what he thought, and then we ate an entire box of ice cream sandwiches and laughed until our stomachs hurt too much.

"Hey." Benji gives Marco a small smile. He doesn't look at the locker. "You doing okay?"

"Been better," Marco says.

Which is more than he said to me, but I understand. Really.

I go back to trying to pick up his stuff just to have something to do, I guess.

"People can totally be the worst sometimes," Benji says. It's not a deep sentence, but I think it's exactly what Marco needs right now. Plus everything Benji says always sounds really smart, because of his accent. "Do you guys know who did this?"

I shake my head. "We just got here. Someone who got out of assembly before we did, I guess. Or went in late." I should have been taking notes. I can tell by the little glance Marco gives me that he thinks I should have been, too. But being responsible for the notebook is hard work. And anyway, he's supposed to be the one noting suspicious activity. I really can't take full responsibility for this.

Guh.

I hate the things I think sometimes.

Marco says, "It could have been an accident. Someone throwing a chair or something. At the general direction of my locker. And hitting nothing else."

"Yeah," Benji says. Softly.

That's when I see a bit of paper folded up on the ground by Marco's locker. I guess it fell out with all of his books. I pick it up and stuff it in my pocket. I'm not super subtle, but Marco is watching Benji, and he doesn't notice. Which is good. For some reason I'm really sure, I don't want him to see this just now.

I just don't think it's good for him to be in charge of this investigation, is what I'm saying.

Benji says, "They need to get security cameras here. At my old school, there were cameras everywhere. Because people were always stabbing each other."

Marco's eyes get big.

"Not really always," he says. "But once." He gives Marco another smile, a little bigger. "I wouldn't worry about any of this, you know? People like to scare other people." He adds, really quietly. "Nothing to be scared of." He offers his fist to Marco.

I see Sasha then, watching us. Or watching Benji. God, is just everyone in love with Benji?

Marco blinks a few times and taps his fist against Benji's, a few seconds too late to not be awkward. Oh, Marco. Even though he and Benji talk a lot, they almost never touch. It's not something Marco's ever mentioned to me, but I can tell it really gets to him whenever they do.

"Can't believe you're leaving soon," Marco says.

"That I am. Soccer camp." He smiles. "And a little tour with the band around London, too."

Marco's eyes are even bigger than when we were talking about people getting stabbed. "Wow, seriously?"

The Floor Is Lava performed at our school dance a few months ago. Most of our class didn't appreciate them, but I was pretty into it. They're a very British invasion band, which I'm weirdly into, I think thanks to my mom who still has a crush on Paul McCartney. They wear skinny ties and sunglasses and they sing so many harmonies that you're worried the songs are going to fall apart, but they never do. Except Benji doesn't sing. Benji, Marco always tells me, with a grin because he thinks it's so endearing, can absolutely not sing.

"I-I mean," Marco says. "You guys are *so* good."

Benji smiles. "Thanks. Just terrible little clubs no one's heard of in London, though, opening for more bands no one's ever heard of. You know, we're playing at the prom on Saturday, at the high school. Did I tell you?"

Marco slowly begins to smile really, really big. "You are?"

"Yup. Right before I leave. Little farewell to America, I guess. Until September. I'll be back."

"But different school from me," Marco says. He's not smiling anymore.

Neither is Benji. "What?"

"He's going to private school," I say. "Prep school."

Marco nods. "Gotta get bred well. Like a puppy."

I guess I must have mentioned to Marco that it sounds like a dog school. Or maybe he figured it out all on his own. Which should probably convince him not to go there, but I guess not.

Benji just says, "Hmm," which I'm guessing wasn't the dramatic reaction Marco was hoping for, but he shakes it off pretty quickly.

He says, "That's awesome about your band, you know? Listen, we've got to get going. Have a great time in Europe. Wave to Italy. I'll go all Italian accent on everyone sometime; we'll take the world by storm."

"I'll see you in a few," Benji says as we go.

"I'm pretty sure he likes you," I tell Marco. "I mean, since he'd have to be living in a box not to notice you're obsessed with him."

"I'm not obsessed. Intrigued. I'm intrigued."

He is so many miles past intrigued.

"We have to get to prom."

"What?"

"I have to get to the prom! I have to get up on stage and tell him I love him in front of *everyone! That's the answer.*"

Only in Marco's head could this ever be the answer to anything. Ever.

Someone snickers and makes some weird gesture at us as he goes by. I guess it's dirty. I don't even know anymore.

I say, "That's the worst idea I've ever heard."

He squawks. "What?"

It's not like I can tell him he's crazy, and that there's a decent possibility he's going to get his heart broken in front of the entire high school graduating class who I know from my brother Brian are mostly cutthroat jerk-weasels. I can't ever mention the possibility that maybe Benji's just stroking his own ego by flirting with someone he knows adores him. Or that even if Benji does like him, most people aren't really crazy about huge dramatic gestures the way Marco is.

Because he sounds so happy. And this is Marco, and this is how he works. Marco is not all that great at the day-to-day. And if Benji can't handle it, then at least Marco will know that it wouldn't have worked out anyway.

"Because how are we going to get into the prom? We're eighth graders."

Marco gives me a smile to rival Benji's. "When have we ever not figured something out?"

While he's chattering to himself, working on plans that will never work, I stealthily unfold the note in my pocket and take a look.

DIE.

I look at Marco, but he has no idea what's going on.

SHERRI'S SOCK AND OTHER
NATURAL DISASTERS

And then there are yearbooks and sixth-grade girls hugging each other and crying and Marco has his meeting with Dr. Slade and I wait around outside the office and then the day's over, and so is middle school. I don't have anyone to say any sentimental goodbyes to, since I'll see everyone at graduation and a bunch of them at Hebrew school in two hours, but I expect to have to wait because I figure Marco has to do some tortured awkward goodbye with Benji. He doesn't. He waves and gives Benji the same smile he gives anyone else, and then we're out to the bus stop.

"That was weird," I say.

"Have to be stealthy. I can't even remember what bus we get on. This is horrible. Why do all the buses look the same?"

I say, "Remember when we were in elementary school, and they all had colors? And they'd call, like, *the purple bus is here.*"

"They were all really the same color."

"But they had signs on the sides of them. The purple bus. The yellow bus."

"They were all yellow, though, really." He's not having any of this, apparently. I guess it's that time of the day when Marco starts getting cranky about how he's staying at my house. He's with me for at least another week, until his parents get home from Japan. They go there a lot, and he usually stays with us and doesn't complain about it. But this time is different, because this time they're coming back with a baby.

I've at least figured out that Marco doesn't want to talk about it. My mom hasn't. She's always bringing it up at dinner, how Mrs. Kimura just e-mailed her another picture of the baby and isn't she *precious,* and has Marco gone through Robbie's old clothes and figured out if there's anything that might fit her, and (while she's covering my little siblings' ears) does he really think that kind of language will be appropriate once his new sister is here?

Pretty much the second we're off the bus and through the front door, Mom's yelling, "I just got off the phone with your mother, Marco." She has my tiny brother Robbie sitting on the counter next to the sink, and she's scrubbing at his cheek like she's trying to sand the whole thing off. "She says they're making sure they get all their sightseeing done before it's time to pick up your sister! Stephen, what on earth happened to your hair?"

"I match Robbie," I say, because Robbie is currently purple. "My shirt, too."

"Sightseeing is a lame and redundant phrase, and I hate my mom for using it." Marco goes straight to the fridge and hides his head in it. He's been sort of a jerk since he's been staying here. My mom keeps telling me it's normal, but I'm still worried she's going to blame me for it, and sooner or later she's going to assault me with a lecture about how I should have better friends. She's already hinted at that a million times. She says things like, "Maybe Marco doesn't respect you as much as he should." Dad used to turn it all into this big song and dance about how I let people push me around, and I need to get tougher or something.

Whatever.

Anyway, I don't really care when Marco pushes me around when we're alone, but it's different and weird when it's in front of my mom.

I don't think she has any idea what kind of a delicate balance we're in that's keeping Marco from gnawing us both into pieces, because she keeps chattering on about Mr. and Mrs. Kimura's journey through Japan. Marco's totally tuned her out and is busy frowning into a bowl of cereal, so I try to figure out what exactly this blue stuff is all over my brother.

"Blueberry juice," Mom tells me. "Look at this," and then she pulls up the hem of his shirt. It makes a *shuck* sound when she peels it away from his stomach. He's totally covered. He's like that girl from *Charlie and the Chocolate Factory*. He's turning into a blueberry.

Robbie smiles at me.

"And we need to be out the door in twenty," Mom says. "I don't care if I have to paint the rest of him to match."

"So yummy," Robbie says.

"Is Brian taking us?" I say. Brian is the oldest. He's going away to college in the fall. Which is too scary to even think about. Everybody's always going places now, it seems like.

I start messing up Robbie's hair with both of my hands, and he giggles.

Mom says, "Hate to disappoint, but you're in the mom-mobile today."

I don't know why she says mom-mobile. And all my friends' moms do, too. I wonder if they know the other ones do it.

"Brian's bringing Julia to tryouts," Mom says. "Robbie, give me that face."

"It's *my* face!"

"I wanted Brian…" I say, but Mom gives me a look, so I shut up. I totally forgot about Julia's tryouts, too. I'm the worst. But it's hard to keep track of what's going on with everyone. Marco can't even keep track of how many of us there are.

"I need to change," I say.

"No kidding." Mom looks at Marco. "Marco, you're probably going to want to put on a nicer shirt, honey."

Marco picks his head up. It's like he just remembered we're all here. "Where are we going?"

I attack Robbie's cheek with a paper towel. "Hebrew school."

"Again?"

"Yeah, Wednesdays and Fridays."

"We *just* went."

I say, "Yeah, on Wednesday…"

Mom says, "You can run errands with me if you'd rather, sweetie. Boring ones, though. Bank, pick up prescriptions, grab some groceries if I have time, return that shirt Sherri thought she wanted..."

"Ugly shirt," I say.

"She said she wanted it. God only knows."

Marco says, "I can't stay here?"

Mom says, "No, you're not old enough, babe." I really don't know where she gets these rules. Sasha's mom lets her baby-sit, and I'm not allowed home alone. But usually either Julia or Brian is here anyway, so I don't mind.

Except it seems like Brian's never around anymore. So maybe I should freak out about this rule and make Mom change it. I can't remember the last time I freaked out about something.

"Is Brian here?" I say.

Mom wets a fresh paper towel and rubs it over Robbie's mouth. "I don't think he's home yet. He went somewhere after school and he's picking Julia up... if he's late she's going to have his head."

Marco says, "I stay home alone at my house all the time."

Robbie swings his feet all wildly while Mom's pawing at his face, and he gets me right in the chest with his tiny rock-hard foot. Marco pushes me back up when I stumble. I don't know how he got here that fast.

"Sorry," Robbie says.

I say, "It's cool. Superhero Marco."

Robbie watches him. "Yeah. Superhero."

Mom finishes with Robbie and sets him on the floor. "You can go to Hebrew school with Stephen or you can come run errands with me."

Marco pouts his way over to the sink and rinses out his cereal bowl. I'm about to tell him to stop being such a jerk when my little sister Sherri runs in and collides with my legs. She's wearing her soccer uniform, which is completely bizarre, because she didn't even have soccer practice today.

She must see that I'm confused, because she says, "It's show-and-tell day, duh."

"Oh."

"I can't find my sock," she says. One of her feet is naked inside the sneaker, the other isn't.

"Did you ask Julia?" Even though Sherri's like eight years younger than Julia, Mom's always getting their stuff mixed up.

"Marco." I smack his shoulder. "Are you hearing this? Missing sock."

Marco lights up. "I'll make a list of suspects!"

I let him borrow the camera so he can take a picture of Sherri's mismatched feet.

"This is your job," Marco says.

"Yeah, well." Because what am I supposed to say, *That's only for real cases, and we haven't done a missing sock case since we were seven?*

Mom says, "Stephen, what is Rabbi Feldman going to say if you're late?" My Bar Mitzvah was supposed to be a few months ago, but then my parents got divorced and we pushed it back until September. Ever since I accidentally mentioned to Mom that I'm the only Jewish kid in my grade who isn't a Bar Mitzvah, she's convinced I have to keep proving to the rabbi that I'm dedicated or whatever. Which is dumb, because it's not like everyone doesn't know why I haven't had my Bar Mitzvah. It's not like anyone's blaming me.

Plus Rabbi Feldman likes my mom so much that if I don't watch out I'm probably going to turn into Stephen Feldman.

Marco says, "Show her your ankles, Sherri."

Sherri pushes her feet out and looks up at Mom with the world's most desperate face.

Mom says, "Sherri, you don't have another pair of clean socks?"

"That's a *waste* of this sock!" Marco says. "That's an entire sock whose purpose in life won't be fulfilled for who knows how long. That's a whole extra sock in the laundry that she didn't even get to wear. And who knows how long this sock will go from the washing machine to her drawer and back without ever finding its mate. Do you have any idea how much water you could be wasting by not—"

Mom says, "You have ten minutes."

Marco's already running up the stairs, yelling, "I'll start interviewing suspects!"

Mom gives me a look. "Get your sisters ready, please?"

"Uh-huh." I jerk my head at Sherri so she'll follow me and start the exciting process of herding her upstairs. She figures out pretty quickly that she and Marco are on their own on the sock thing, and she glares at me like she doesn't know who I am.

I shut her in her room. "Get ready."

"Traitor."

It's too bad I'm on her bad side, honestly, because Sherri really is useful for actual detective stuff. I should hire her as a new assistant, now that Julia decided she's too mature for that.

Although really, with Marco changing schools, what I'm going to need is a new partner.

Okay, so what I'm really going to need is a new boss, I guess.

The shirt I want to change into isn't in my room, so I trek back downstairs to the laundry room. I'm at the end of the hallway, so I pass each of my siblings' doors on the way.

Marco made me do a whole section on my siblings in the case file like a month ago. I added a ton of good details and insider information on where they hide their diaries and their money, but Marco said, "I'm just trying to keep track of how many there are, God." So at the bottom of the page, in really tiny, bored letters, I wrote, *Brian: 18, Julia: 15, Stephen: 13, Sherri: 8, Catherine: 5, Robbie: 3.* Marco stared at it for a while and then shook his head. "Ridiculous." Like he'd really never believed how many of us there were until then. We've been friends since before Catherine and Robbie were born.

We stop by the laundry room, where Mom's coaxing Robbie into his dress pants. He's still at that age where he looks younger when he's dressed up than when he's running around in a T-shirt and a Pull-Up. He's only going to the kiddie synagogue class with Catherine, but Mom likes to make him look nice. Impressing the rabbi and all that.

"Mom?" I say.

She doesn't look up. "I haven't seen the sock since

yesterday morning at the latest. But I'll let you know if I come across any further evidence."

I came to ask about the shirt, but whatever. "Do you have an alibi?"

"I was with Robbie the whole time."

Robbie nods.

I say, "Thank you, both of you. Your cooperation is much appreciated."

Robbie salutes me. He's a champ.

My shirt is hanging from the doorknob. I bring it upstairs and run right into Julia. Actually, right into the enormous book Julia's holding. She's really tall, at least five inches taller than me, so she's some kind of crazy giant with a textbook bludgeoning tool when she's two steps above me. She cut all her hair off a few weeks ago. We all begged her not to do it, but it looks totally awesome, it turns out.

She holds up a hand before I can say anything. She hasn't looked up from her book. The cover says ALGEBRA II.

Here's the thing about Julia. When she was in eighth grade and I was in sixth, all my friends suddenly wanted to have sleepovers at my house instead of theirs, and I didn't really get it until my mom caught a bunch of them trying to sneak up to Julia's room. Marco was the one who finally said, "Stephen, she's really, really pretty."

The other thing about Julia is she's my favorite, and she's the only girl Marco has ever, ever loved.

"Marco already interviewed me," she says.

"Interrogated."

"Whatever. I know nothing about the sock. And my tryouts are in half an hour, and they're twenty minutes away, and *if Brian doesn't get here in the next four minutes and twenty seconds I swear to God—*"

The last thing about Julia is that she's tried out for math camp every summer and hasn't gotten in. This is the last year before she's too old, and I'm scared that if she doesn't make it this time, she's going to throw herself in front of a bus.

"Good luck," I say. "Don't worry about the sock. It's under control."

"Glad to hear it."

Sherri's outside my room, still not dressed for Hebrew school, of course, demanding to know what I've learned from Mom and Julia.

"Where's Marco?" I say.

She points inside my room. "He's a bad detective."

"Shhh." I send her to investigate in Brian's room, then

I go to dig through my drawers, in case Sherri demands for me to prove my own innocence. All the lights are off in my room, and Marco's lying on the bed with his arm over his eyes. He looks like he's suffering from some terrible illness in an old movie.

"Does your head hurt?"

"Julia seems innocent," he tells me. He doesn't move his arm, but he's talking in his normal voice, so he's probably fine.

I say, "I know."

"It's very hard to think of a good plan," he says.

"About Benji?"

"Yes. Benji. Nothing else in the whole world but Benji." He sounds so tired. He sits on the edge of the bed and dangles his legs. Julia might be way taller than me, but I'm way taller than Marco. He's the shortest kid in our grade. That's something he tries not to think about.

"I'm going to think of a plan," he says. "We're getting to the prom. I just need time to think, and we're going to stupid Hebrew school..."

"I thought I was going to help think of a plan. Just after Hebrew school, okay?"

"Yeah, okay. I'll let you know if I need help."

Sherri runs in. "Brian still isn't here, and I didn't find my sock in his room."

I say, "Only one suspect left, then."

Like she can read my mind, Mom calls from downstairs, "Julia, can you get Catherine down here?"

"I'm *studying*!" Julia screams.

Mom yells, "Stephen?"

"I'm on it."

Marco flops back down on the bed. "Why is everyone always *yelling* at your house?"

"What?"

"You guys are always *yelling* at each other."

Marco is the loudest person I know. I'm not about to argue about it, but I'm just saying. He could win an award. I'm pretty sure he did, when we had paper plate awards in elementary school.

Besides, we're not always yelling. And we're definitely not yelling *at* each other.

I head down the hall to check on Catherine. She's on her bed. Sherri's sock is on her hand. She's pretending it's a puppet. It's talking to her. She gives me a big smile without stopping her sock conversation. That's talent. Catherine might end up kind of cool.

Mom screams my name, I order Catherine into her

dress and shoes like some kind of drill sergeant. She thinks it is hilarious, which wasn't at all my plan, but it works out.

We're almost ten minutes late for Hebrew school. Mom's way more angry about this than the rabbi. Marco and I sneak in, and he spends the whole hour sulking in the corner. And it's a pretty cool day, too. We're working with the little kids, helping them color and cut out pages in their Hebrew workbooks. But Marco won't even pick up a crayon. He's more stubborn than even that six-year-old Jared, who will do anything to lick the markers.

I finally give Marco the notebook just so he'll have something to do, and he starts scribbling in it pretty frantically after a while. But he's still sulking.

"What's up with your friend?" this girl Rachel asks me. Rachel has more hair than anyone I've ever seen.

"He sucks," I mumble. And I immediately feel bad about saying it, but seriously, I'm trying to think of a way to help him woo the guy of his dreams, and he can't even sit through Hebrew school for me? The stuff I ask him to do . . . it's not like it's hard.

JULIA (AND ALSO BRIAN)

The school counselor, Miss Bernstein, who Marco swears has a crush on Benji, must have called while we were at Hebrew school, because when Mom picks us up she knows about Marco's locker being bashed in. And I think she also knows some of the other stuff, notes and things. And also maybe about the snow cone.

She lets Marco sit in the front on the way home, and I hang in the back with Sherri and Catherine and Robbie. The little ones are asleep, and Sherri gets that something serious is going on, so it's weirdly quiet.

"I'm so sorry that happened to you, sweetheart," Mom says.

Marco shrugs and doesn't say anything.

I'm really not trying to be a jerk here, but I'm the one with blue hair, and while Marco gets "sweetheart," and the front seat, I get my little sister drooling on my shoulder.

Mom says, "You take it easy tonight, okay?" She checks the rearview mirror and then smiles at Marco a little. "Just making sure Robbie's asleep so he won't hear me tell you I got ice cream at the store."

Marco gives her a weak grin back.

Mom lets it drop after that, though. And I wait until we've hauled the groceries inside and Mom's gone upstairs to interrogate him about it. I get that he doesn't want to talk about this stuff, but we're not supposed to keep important information under wraps. It goes against our whole operation.

I say, "You didn't tell me Miss Bernstein talked to you today. I thought you were with Dr. Slade the whole time."

"No. She barged in and made me talk to her." He groans when I hand him a stack of plates, but he gives in and helps me set the table. I check what's in the Crock-Pot and I can't even tell what it is, but usually that's a good sign with Crock-Pot stuff.

Marco says, "Everyone is very concerned for my

well-being. They can see that I am a boy head over heels. That's why Miss Bernstein was there. She and Dr. Slade, and really anyone who's interacted with me in the past few hours, they can all see the brilliance of my plan in my eyes, and they're trying to buddy up to me before I'm world famous for my Romantic Gesture of Awesome. Miss Bernstein is probably trying to steal my tactics so that she can woo Benji for her own means. Nice try, Miss Bernstein. Nice try."

"So it had nothing to do with your locker at all." I know it does. I'm being facetious, as my mother would say. *Facetious* is one of those words I know how to use in a sentence but not what it actually means.

He puts down a fork. "It's kind of stupid how much they're fussing over me. They keep telling us that when we're in high school, no one's going to baby-sit us anymore. We need to get ready. Cold cruel world. So on and so forth. And here they are giving me a group hug because someone drop-kicked my locker."

"Roundhouse, probably."

"Whatever."

"I don't want to talk about high school."

Marco shrugs. He used to not want to, either. Every time someone brought it up, he'd cover his ears and sing.

He actually celebrated when my Bar Mitzvah was postponed, because it meant I'd be a kid for longer. Even though he'd already bought a suit.

Now all of a sudden he's looking forward to high school, to this growing up thing. All of a sudden when we're not doing it together.

Catherine is trying to climb up me from behind. Marco watches me, not even pretending he's not disgusted. After I did potty-training duty with Robbie this morning, he treated me like a biohazard until I showered. I should tell him that the real thing that's going to make him grow up is the new baby, not high school. Then we'll see how excited he is about not being a kid anymore.

I'm so excited to meet his little sister that I can't really stand it. But I've seen Marco be a stubborn idiot about a thousand things, and he seems to be going for a record with this one. His parents started talking about adopting from Japan over a year ago, and Marco has been a bratty mess about it ever since.

Mom comes into the kitchen holding all the groceries we dumped by the door. She stops to give Marco a kiss on the head. He pretends to wince, but I can tell he kind of likes it. His family's not very touchy-feely, but he kind of is, ("Embrace me, Stephen!" This kid is so weird.) so

I try to keep that in mind and hug him sometimes when I don't feel like it, like I have to do with Sherri sometimes. Mom's good at telling when to touch.

In the living room, Sherri turns the TV on super loud, and Mom yells in that Robbie's napping. Sherri doesn't turn it down.

"Are Brian and Julia home?" I say.

She nods.

"So everyone's accounted for," I say. "Except for Catherine." I pick her up by her shoulders. "I found this, though. Is this Catherine?"

She giggles. She's still sleepy.

"Don't hold her like that!" Mom calls over her shoulder while she puts tomatoes in the fridge. "You'll pull her arms off."

Catherine looks up at me with this shocked face. I shake my head at her.

Mom says, "We're going to eat a little late, I think. I want to cook some of this corn. It's beautiful. And it's Julia's favorite . . ."

Her tryout. Right. "How did it go?"

Mom breathes out, long and slow. "She didn't get in."

"Noooo," Marco moans.

Mom does another one of those slow breaths. "She's

pretty crushed. She doesn't want to come downstairs. Stephen, you want to give me a hand here?"

It's one of those questions that only has one answer, especially since I'm done setting the table, and Mom's looking for an excuse to make me stop manhandling Catherine. I start putting bags of chips away.

"She studied this whole month," Marco says. "This isn't fair."

Mom says, "It's not the least bit fair, you're right. God knows she tried as hard as she could. But...don't forget that your sister is blessed in other ways. She can tell a joke that's a hundred times funnier than anything your father has ever said, and, well, that face of hers...Julia has so many amazing qualities."

She's just not smart. Mom didn't say it, but it's pretty much as if she did.

I say, "But she worked really hard."

"And that's what we need to keep in mind, and why we need to be so proud of her. Because she tried."

I guess. But I'm good at math, and so's Mom. And I get As and Bs without even trying, while Julia spends three hours a night on her homework and still barely makes Cs. It's hard to be proud of her when it makes her so sad.

"Where's my brother?" I say.

"Big or little?"

"Big."

"I don't know. He brought Julia home, but she said he left right after."

"Is he coming home for dinner?"

"Don't know, sweetie."

I've hardly seen Brian this whole week. He's with his girlfriend all the time. When he is home, he's rushing around jingling his keys, like he's always in a hurry. Like he thinks he has to gather us all up before we can go. Mom always does the key-jingling thing when she's trying to get us all out the door. But it's not like Brian brings us wherever he's going. "Maybe he's going out with Jessica," I say.

He's been dating this girl Jessica Brewin for like forever, but I don't even know her that well. She plays tennis, and she's going to UPenn like Brian, and she's going to major in biology. And Brian says she makes the world's best lemon bars. That's all I have on her in my notebook. Oh, and also her dad is the head of the school board, and I don't know exactly what it means, but it makes me really, really nervous whenever Jessica's around. Like she's going to report me if my shirt isn't tucked in or something.

I don't know why they even want to see each other all the time now that they know each other that well. She's probably sick of him.

Mom says, "Mmm. He is out a lot. Ever since your father left...I'm worried about him."

Marco looks at me and then quickly back down. I don't know what that meant. I wonder if I can do that—just give people a glance like that and make them feel like they missed something. I don't think I can do that. I wish I could. I wish I could do anything but shake my head a little and ask Mom, "You're worried about Dad?"

I don't like the way the word *Dad* sounds, even though that's still what I call him in my head. Julia calls him The Sperm Whale. I should pick that up.

Mom gives me a weird look. "No."

"About Bri. Got it. I'm stupid, sorry. Julia must be contagious."

"Stephen," Mom says, and Marco gives me a completely different look this time. I understand this one.

I say, "Sorry sorry sorry sorry."

Marco's still frowning at me. "Not funny."

Yeah, well, not cool. I say, "Whoa, do not tell me what I can say about my sister." Because seriously, I can't believe he said that. Okay, maybe it *wasn't* funny, but it isn't Marco's place to tell me. There is nothing, not anything I hate as much in the entire world as someone trying to tell me how I'm supposed to treat my siblings. If it's from Mom, fine, but when one of Julia's friends gets involved when we're fighting or that lady from our synagogue tells me I shouldn't give Robbie candy before dinner, I always think I'm going to Hulk out and rip off my shirt and rip a chasm in the earth especially for them. They don't know us. Let us have our world.

I've never felt like that about Marco before. Ever. And I think I have felt about every kind of angry in the whole world at Marco at some point or another, but not this one.

And even though he can tell I'm boiling lava mad, he doesn't apologize. So I do what I always do when Marco makes me mad. I take a deep breath in, and then I breathe it all out. I force all the anger out of my lungs and onto the floor.

Done.

After all the groceries are put away, though, Marco offers to help Mom with the cooking, which I guess should make me happy, since it gets me out of it. But I know he's doing it because he loves to cook, and not because he's trying to make me happy.

I go upstairs. I write "YOU ARE AWESOME—S" on a Post-it note and leave it on Julia's door. But that just makes me angrier. I was planning to do it before Marco said anything, but now it's hard to convince myself that I'm not doing it because I feel guilty. And I'm *not*.

Julia's great.

Anyway, maybe she'll think it's a note from Sherri.

I stop at Brian's room and knock, even though I know he's not there. After a few seconds, I open the door and peek in.

He made the bed before he left.

I wish he were here. Brian and I used to be way close, even though he's five years older than I am. We played pirates, which I guess everyone does, but our version was way better. There are these two oak trees really close to each other in our backyard, and we made up a pirate ship that spanned both of them. To get from the bow to the stern, you had to climb from the branch of one tree over to the branches of the other. Which was scary enough when the enemies *weren't* trying to shoot cannonballs through our ship. And they usually were.

But then Brian got old, and I guess that's all that happened. I'm not mad at him for growing up, the way Sasha got mad at her big sister. It was more like he got mad at me for staying a kid.

Anyway, I'm growing up now, so maybe that will fix things.

I don't know.

He's never liked Marco. Maybe that was another

problem we had. He thinks Marco's a jerk. And . . . yeah, he is sometimes. But Marco also remembers something I said I wanted six months ago and gets it for me for my birthday, and he writes comics about what I missed and leaves them in my locker and does all my homework for days I stay home sick. He's the first person I want to tell all my good news, and I'm the first person he tells, too. And when Tabitha got that horrible haircut and Luke was making fun of her, Marco hugged Tabitha and told her she was the prettiest girl he'd ever seen, and then he punched Luke in the face.

All of this is on Marco's page in the very back of the detective notebook. The part I don't let him see. And I definitely wouldn't let Brian see it, because he would say something about how it's telling that I need a list to remind me of the good things about my best friend.

Maybe I just like lists.

I walk into Brian's room and sit on the bed. The springs creak under me. We all got new mattresses a few years ago, but Brian wouldn't let us replace his. He doesn't like change.

He has two prom tickets on his nightstand. I want to take a picture, but if Marco found out, he'd totally suggest stealing them, and there's no way I'm going to let our mission get in the way of Brian's prom. He's been talking about it practically nonstop for like a month. He's been poring over pictures of flowers that match Jessica's dress. He's such a goober sometimes.

I reach into my pocket for my camera to take a picture, just because a picture of prom tickets would go well in our case file, when this is all said and done. Marco will be mad that I didn't steal the tickets, but whatever, that's later-Stephen's problem, and how angry can he really get about it once the mission's over?

I pull the camera out of my pocket and out comes the note from Marco's locker.

And then there's nothing to stop my mind from going too fast, here in this room all alone, just me and this note.

The thing is, it's hard to stay angry at Marco, because so often I'm just scared for him.

Which is stupid. Because nothing's going to happen to Marco, because I'm here and I'm a good sidekick.

I take a picture of the prom tickets. I'll make sure Marco doesn't see it until the prom is over. That will be my mission. That's what I'll worry about.

EVERYTHING IS ACCOUNTED FOR

Julia eats dinner by herself upstairs. After Marco retreats to my room and I finish helping Mom and Sherri clear the table, I grab a brownie from the pantry and knock on her door.

"Yeah?" she calls, and I can tell she was crying but isn't anymore.

"Me."

"Hey. You can come in."

She's sitting on her bed with her laptop open and playing some soft music I don't recognize. She turns it off, even though she doesn't have to talk. "Brownie?" she says.

"Yep. Store-bought."

"Doesn't matter. Come split it with me."

I sit on the foot of her bed and bend it in half. Crumbs get pretty much everywhere. I look at her, and she shrugs. Brian would totally freak out if I got crumbs on his bed. Julia and Brian are the least alike of any of my siblings, so it doesn't make much sense that they're my favorites.

"I'm sorry about the thing," I say.

She chews and shakes her head. "I don't want to talk about it."

"Oh."

"Talk about something else."

I guess that puts me on the spot, because that's the only explanation for why I just blurt out, "I think someone's out to get Marco."

"What?"

"That someone maybe is going to try to hurt him.

I hear footsteps running down the hallway and downstairs, then immediately back upstairs.

"What is that?" Julia says.

"Marco. I've got to go."

"*There* you are." Marco appears in Julia's doorway. "I need you. Come on. Hey, Julia. I love you, y'know? Wait, do you need him?"

She gives him this little smile and shakes her head. "No, he's all yours. Want some brownie?"

"Can't eat chocolate. Migraines. Stephen, Stephen come on."

I leave Julia the rest of my brownie and follow Marco down the hall. "I finished the plan," he says.

"For the prom?"

"For the prom. Come on." He flops down on the inflatable mattress and leans back against the side of my bed. He kicks his pajamas out of the way to make room for me. He still wears pajamas with spaceships on them, and I'm pretty sure they used to be mine. Mom sometimes gives Mrs. Kimura my hand-me-downs, since Robbie's ages away from using them. Mrs. Kimura tells Marco they're from his older cousin. If Marco notices he's wearing the same shirt I wore last year, he doesn't mention it.

I sit down next to him, and he takes our—my— detective notebook out of his pocket.

"How'd you get that?" I took it back after Hebrew school, where I told him exactly what page he could write on and watched him like a hawk. There's stuff in there that isn't his. About old investigations and stuff. About him. About Dad.

And there's the new photo of Brian's nightstand that I'm going to need to print and put in there, but that can wait, I guess.

Marco says, "I had to use all my expert detective skills. I interviewed witnesses, dusted for fingerprints, tore through pages and pages of police reports on my suspects, and finally discovered that the notebook was, in fact, in your backpack."

"Shut up."

"I added to Benji's section. Look."

I find the page. I skip over certain stuff really quickly, just like always. Yeah, the stuff about Dad.

Marco must be really psyched about his plan, because his writing is humongous. He took up three pages with this. I'm trying to hide that I'm irritated by that.

THE GREAT PROM HEIST

"Heist…" I say.

"It seemed appropriate," Marco says.

"No, it's good. It's really good."

Now I'm thinking about this whole prom thing in a different way. Before, it was another one of Marco's stupid schemes, like the time he tried to steal all the yellow

Jell-O powder from the cafeteria so they couldn't make it ever, ever again.

Now it's a heist. We've done schemes before, but we've never, ever done a heist. We weren't ready before.

But I think after our last major investigation, we've proven we're master detectives. Even if that investigation didn't end the way anyone wanted, we still solved the mystery.

I hate the Sperm Whale.

We were just trying to figure out why he was sneaking out all the time. And then we wanted to know where he was going. And once we found him, we wanted to know who he was with. And then who that lady was. And then what they were doing.

And then we left the case report on Mom's pillow, because we're detectives, and we have integrity, and that's what we had to do. Marco said we didn't have to, but I thought we did. Because right then, having integrity was the only thing that made any sense.

And everything happened kind of fast after that.

I really should have listened to Marco, and I think maybe I'm going to be thinking that for a million different reasons until the day I die.

Anyway, we solved that mystery. And now we're ready

for a heist. A good one. Because after this, who even knows. This might be our last big mission.

I say, "Except I think *heist* means robbery. And we're not stealing anything."

"We're stealing a young man's heart. And a few other things. Keep reading."

SATURDAY MORNING: HEIST PREPARATION
$100 each
- Marco: Accomplished. Parents left emergency money with son before betraying him with ill-advised trip to Japan. We have decided that this does, in fact, qualify as an emergency.
- Stephen: will need to obtain his through alternate means.
  - Luke Gorman: (Boooo. Jerkweasel.)
  - Has parents who are rich but strict (and therefore controlling of his electronics purchases)
  - Is Desperately Seeking iPod
  - Marco has deduced that Luke would definitely pay $50 for iPod, especially considering that said iPod, before being

given to Stephen For his thirteenth birthday, is loaded with Marco's impressive music collection (including, For the record, The Floor Is Lava's new EP, though Luke will likely not appreciate it as Luke is the enemy oF all that is good and true).

- Has been known to play basketball at the McKinley Middle School outdoor courts on Saturday aFternoons. Marco has already texted him and conFirmed that he will be there with the money tomorrow.
- Stephen must have another $50 somewhere. I mean really.

"I do." I look up at him. "But I'm not selling the iPod."

"You never even use it."

But Marco gave it to me. It was the only birthday present he ever guessed wrong. I'm just really attached to my beat-up CD player. Maybe I'm more like Brian than I thought. I hope so.

Marco says, "This is a good way to get some use out of the iPod. The only downside is that Luke profits. Which is why I'm planning to put the entire *Sound of Music* soundtrack on there. Three times. With the names disguised."

I laugh, but just a little. The truth is, I get uncomfortable whenever Marco talks about Luke, because there's a lot there that I don't understand. Marco and Luke were friends, best friends, when they were really little kids, before my family even moved here. And Marco didn't even tell me that until really recently. For as long as I've known them, they've hated each other. But they're still on strange terms about some things—like, it isn't weird that Marco has his number and that Luke answers his texts, even though it should be, and Marco answers Luke's texts in five seconds, I've seen him—and Luke is the only, only person that can boss Marco around, and yeah, I'm a little jealous of that sometimes. It always seems like Marco really wants to impress Luke, or to please him, I guess. Like Luke is a tough teacher and Marco doesn't want to fail the class.

But these are all guesses I've made on my own, because Marco will never, ever talk about Luke. "It's just easiest to do it this way," is the most he's ever told me.

He says, "Why are you all frowning on me? I'm serious about *The Sound of Music*. Your mother has it. I checked. Too bad we don't have time to go to my house. My mother has it in Italian."

"You really don't care if I sell it?"

"You're doing it to *help* me, remember? It's okay." He reaches a hand up and messes up my hair.

"You sure?"

"Sure I'm sure, Stevey. Keep reading."

Permission letter from Dr. Slade.

Marco says, "This took me ages to figure out. No matter how awesome we look—and wait 'til you get to that part of the heist, 'cause we're going to look awesome—we don't have high school IDs. I thought maybe we could steal them from your brother and someone, but—"

"—I don't look like Brian."

He nods and tucks some hair behind his ear. "And nobody in the world looks like me. So what we need is a written letter of permission. And the only authority we have to exploit is Dr. Slade. Unless you think you can steal paperwork from your brother's girlfriend's dad or whatever."

"I don't see that happening."

"That's what I thought. So Dr. Slade's our best bet."

"How are we going to get the stationery?"

"Keep reading, keep reading."

- Enlist the help of Sasha.
- This is all Stephen. Say whatever you always say that makes her eyes go all melty.
- Sasha is middle school president and has a key to Dr. Slade's secretary's (hereafter "Miss Larson") office in order to retrieve and deposit minutes from the student government meetings. While she cannot get into Mr. Slade's office itself, judging Dr. Slade's signature that—if you'll excuse the stereotyping—looks quite more feminine on some of those letters he sends out than others, Miss Larson occasionally writes notes in his stead and will likely have some of his stationery in the vicinity. Also, Marco investigated this and it is true. He is very smart.

"This part is almost too easy." Marco takes his phone off my nightstand and scrolls through the pictures. "I took this while I was in the office today. Look. The attendance book goes right next to the folder with his stationery in it. Could not be easier for her to grab a sheet while she's putting the book away."

"Print that picture for the file."

"I will, I will. God, you act like I'm stupid sometimes, Stephen."

"Do I really make Sasha's eyes go ... like you said?"

He makes this exasperated noise but doesn't answer.

- On Saturdays at 3 p.m., Sasha is the assistant coach of a pre-kindergarten soccer team that practices on the McKinley Middle School Field. Once informed of our plan, she can leave to "get a drink of water," retrieve stationery, and hand said stationery off to Stephen while Marco is completing the iPod transaction.
- Enlist the help of Julia.
- Marco and/or Stephen will fill Julia in on our plan. Probably Marco, because Julia likes him more.
- Julia is a romantic and will find this all very adorable, though really this is not adorable, due to its being a matter of life and/or death.
- Julia is friends with pretty much everyone at Taft High School. She can ask around and text people or pull whatever strings she needs to find out what teachers will be supervising the prom. She will create a character profile on said teacher and deliver it to us at McKinley Middle

school before we depart following the iPod/
stationery exchanges.

"You're not giving her a lot of time," I say.

"There's another step in this objective. We'll need her notes well ahead of the actual heist."

I say, "Julia can't spell."

"I'll decipher it. Good thing I'm a genius."

- Enlist the help of Brian.
- We fill Brian in on the plan. Brian has
  perfect handwriting. He will prepare to
  fabricate a note from Dr. Slade to the teacher
  in question, preying on the teacher's
  individual weaknesses and personality traits
  to craft the perfect excuse for why we
  absolutely, completely, definitely need to get
  into the prom. Actual fabrication of this note
  will take place outside of the designated prom
  entry just prior to our attempted (and ultimately
  successful) entrance, once we have obtained the
  stationery and then encountered Brian. But
  that's later.

I look at him. "How are we convincing Brian?"

Marco pulls his bottom lip between his teeth. "I was kind of leaving that part to you."

Eesh. "I'll see what I can do. But start thinking of a Plan B for that one."

"I don't do Plan Bs."

THE HEIST
Transportation

- After a successful trip to McKinley Middle School, where they will exchange money for iPod and romantic favors for stationery, Marco and Stephen enter the school through the entrance in the back of the gym. As per page 14 of notebook (and Figure 9B), please note that the lock on the door has been broken since before April 29th and, as of 2 p.m. June 3rd, has not been repaired.

I flip through the notebook to check. Yep. The man has done his research.

- From school, walk two blocks to Greenly Street bus stop. Catch the 5:52 bus to Tell Road stop, approx. 20 minutes. From there, it is roughly a 10-minute walk to Nic's Discount Tuxedos.

tuxedos

- $100 each will be more than enough to rent one tux apiece. We will look simply stunning.
- Take the 7:16 bus back to school, stash street clothes and backpacks in the boy's locker room—or girl's, if we're feeling unnecessarily gutsy—and take the 7:40 bus from McKinley Middle School to the Myer Street stop. From there, call a cab, and the remaining money will be enough for a cab to the Gold Estate Country Club, where the prom begins at 8 p.m. Because we refuse to arrive at the prom in a bus. That is ridiculous. We will text Brian alerting him of our arrival and he will meet us outside and write us our note.

CONFESS LOVE

- From here, things are best left to the moment. But suffice it to say, I climb onto the stage, hijack the microphone, and confess my love in front of a whole horde of high school strangers. We're both legends. We're legends in love. And everyone lives happily ever after.

This looks so, so much better than Marco's just going up to Benji and telling him he likes him, I have to admit.

Though, to be honest, I'm not exactly sure why he wants me along. Sure, I make a good sidekick, but isn't this a moment for him and Benji, not for him and me?

Unless he's really afraid Benji won't say yes.

I look at him, and I think he reads my mind a little because he says, "Read more," and then he's chewing on the inside of his lip and looking away from me.

- I know there's a good chance he's not in love with me, Stevey. I'm not stupid. I know that maybe I'm not super loveable, and also that maybe he doesn't like boys and even if he does that thirteen is pretty early to be in love with anyone, so I guess I'm a prodigy, too, not just a genius.
- But it's not about that.
- This is why I have to do it like this. Because the point is that he knows. That even if he doesn't like me, he knows that he's amazing and fantastic and that someone likes him a whole, whole lot.
- Anyone can tell someone he likes him, especially when he's about to go away and I'm changing schools. I could do this risk-free. But this is me

showing him I'm taking a real risk. That he's
worth that.

I get it. And it's stupid and loud and kind of embarrassing, but that's how Marco works. This is why he ran upstairs before dinner and mauled Julia with the world's
biggest hug while I was still filling up water glasses. This
is how Marco does love.

Benji should know that, or there's no point.

"So, what do you think?" Marco says.

It's always so weird when Marco wants my approval.

So I try to be honest. But gentle. This isn't the time to
say, *You're right, he probably isn't going to like you back.*

Because really, what are the chances? Things are what
they are. My pretty sister isn't smart enough to go to math
camp, even though it's what she wants more than anything
in the whole world. My dad wasn't out being a secret
agent. He was cheating on my mom. I'm never going to be
anything but Robin to Marco's Batman. And the popular
soccer player rock star isn't going to fall in love with the
tiny wanna-be detective.

And yet we all keep fighting for it. I wonder if it's just
because I'm so tired that this all looks so, so depressing.

But I can honestly say, "It sounds like a lot of fun."

"It will be. 'Cause . . . Stephen?"

"Yeah?"

He smiles. "Nothing." Then he grabs my iPod and puts the earphones in and listens to The Floor Is Lava's EP, and he stays like that until it's time to go to bed.

MARCO'S HEADACHES

He gets them when he's lying awake and can't sleep.

I always hear this long series of whimpers that creep up and down as if he's singing. It always takes me so long to realize that they aren't part of my dream, and I always keep my eyes closed for a few more seconds, as if I want it hard enough, he'll stop and I can go back to sleep.

For some reason, that's always my first thought. That I want to go back to sleep.

I walk to the bathroom in these long, uneven steps. I try to prepare myself before I flick the light switch, but it still feels like someone's shining a flashlight in my eyes. There's a bottle of painkillers in here. I bite one in half. Marco's tiny.

I turn off the light. It's such a relief to be in the dark again that I almost fall asleep right there in the bathroom. But then he whines again.

I sit down at the foot of the air mattress. "Hey. Open your eyes. Doctor Stephen has Tylenol."

He takes these really big pills every morning for the headaches. But then sometimes he gets them anyway, and he's not allowed to take anything stronger than what we gave Robbie when he was teething. It sucks.

"You want me to get Mom?" I ask.

"N-no." He's trying really hard not to cry. I wish there were a way to tell him that it's okay if he cries, that I'll pretend I don't notice.

I say, "Come on, sit up. I brought water."

He starts to sit up, but then he stops and squeezes his head between his hands. He's curled up against the side of my bed like he thinks it's going to give him a hug.

I say, "I should get Mom."

"I don't want your mom."

"Um . . . I could call yours? It's like . . . it's like the middle of the afternoon in Japan, right?"

He doesn't say anything, then he eventually sits all the way up and takes the pill and the water from me. He gulps it down and then leans forward and holds his head. It's too dark to see him very well.

He's probably going to try to sit there, still, until the pill kicks in.

"Come here," I say, and I put an arm around his shoulders. He doesn't move much.

I've been through a few dozen of these headaches with him since he started getting them back in elementary school, but I'm always too half asleep to keep track of how they're supposed to go. And the next time, I'm back at where we started. Taking care of Marco is like the world's worst IQ test.

Eventually he says, "Hurts, Stephen."

"It'll be better in the morning."

"I know."

There's a huge burst of wind outside, and the rain starts coming down hard. It sounds like a million running footsteps. It's been raining since this afternoon, but nothing like this. I was listening to it when I was falling asleep, when it sounded really peaceful.

"Hurts," he whines. He's shaking really hard.

"There's nothing else I can do. You're not allowed to take anything else."

"I *know*."

I take my arm away and close my eyes and lean back against the bed. This whole experience reminds me of sometime this winter, when Catherine and Robbie both had this stomach flu, and all night there were a few of us awake changing rubber sheets and rubbing someone's back.

I say, "Maybe you should tell me about what you're going to say on stage tomorrow."

"No." His voice is rough and tight. "Too soon. Will ruin it."

"You won't ruin it. Just by telling me? Come on."

"I'm gonna ruin it."

He's getting himself all upset, so I try something different. I say, "Okay, how about telling me why you like Benji?" I put my hand on the back of his head.

He laughs a little, then takes a sharp breath in. "We'd be up all night."

"Yeah, well, we're already up."

He looks at me. He keeps clutching his head, but he straightens up a little. "Yeah?"

"Do it."

Marco says, "Um…so…do you remember at the beginning of seventh grade, soccer season, when Benji got hurt at his game? Really hurt, broke his arm in two places. Two totally different places. It's not like they were next to each other."

"I remember him in a cast."

"Yeah. He was just going to kick the ball and this guy tripped him, and he fell so hard, all awkward. It was a foul. The ref called it immediately. But then Benji didn't get up."

Marco goes to every single one of Benji's games. I go to a lot of them, too, but Marco has never missed one.

Marco says, "So his coach ran across the field to him, and me and Tabitha and Lauren, too, and we all kind of crowded around him. Benji was this really awful gray, that slimy gray like paper-mâché. That was all we could really see, because he was curled up and holding his arm and just moaning, and I remember thinking he looked so . . . small."

"God, get your feet off me, they're freezing."

"Put socks on them."

"Are you four? Put your own socks on." I swear I've said this exact same thing to Sherri at some point.

He rubs his forehead and goes, "Please, Stephen? I'm out of socks."

I can't believe I'm doing this. I get up and start digging through my drawer. I'm going to do this by touch. No way I'm turning the lights back on. It would hurt Marco's head, first of all, and I don't want to have to see if he's really as small and gray and cold as his feet make me think. They remind me of the chicken cutlets we have in our freezer. I'm fine just seeing in shadows right now.

Marco is quiet while I pull the socks on. He says, "No one from Benji's family was there. You know, they hardly ever come to his games. Sucks."

"Yeah."

"But the ambulance told him he could take one person, and he said, 'Marco, I want Marco.'" He rubs his head with both hands. "So I went with him. And I stayed with him the whole time we were there. Like four hours. And I went and got the nurse when he was thirsty, and let him beat me at checkers, and held his hand when they were setting the bone. I was like his right-hand man the whole day."

"Right-hand. Heh."

Marco looks at me in this way I can tell is probably very serious. He's definitely not laughing. "Except he broke his left arm," he says. "Not his right. So he already had a right hand. So your pun is lame."

"You're a jerk when your head hurts."

"I know. At the end of it, right before my mom got

there to pick me up, he gave me this hug. He could only do it with one arm, but he hugged me *hard*. So hard it hurt a little. My favorite part was when some doctor asked if I was his brother." He looks at me, and I can see his smile taking over his whole face. "And he said, '*No. No way. That is not my brother at all.*'"

"Yeah, I totally don't follow."

"Head *hurts*."

"What do you think I can do about it?"

He turns away from me and wraps his arms around his head. "That's a really important story. I didn't tell anyone. Both of us, we... it was like we both dreamed it. We never talked about it. We're friends and all, but that was... that day was different. Like an alternate reality."

I say, "So you like him because of one day?"

"No. Why are you being like that? I like him because he completely trusted me and depended on me and wasn't embarrassed about it, and it's like this secret we both know. And he wanted *me* and not because I'm like his brother. Not because I'm like his brother at all."

I guess that shouldn't surprise me, considering how Marco feels about being someone's brother. But I kind of wonder if he's like mine. It isn't anything I've ever thought about before. But now I'm hearing him talking about

Benji, and I know that me and Marco are so, so not like him and Benji, but what are we, because we're not even going to be together next year, and he's sitting here with a headache and I don't even know how to take care of him. And Marco knew how to take care of a broken arm. When that broken arm was Benji's.

I guess I don't know if Marco would take care of me like that. Not if Benji were in the room, and he could look at him instead.

I guess I don't know what happens to me if Benji actually does like Marco. If that means Benji won't just be the boy he has a crush on, or won't just be his boyfriend, even, but if he'll be his best friend, too.

Except he'll have a new best friend at his new school anyway, so I don't even know why I'm thinking about this.

Someone else will sit up with him through migraines and probably won't wish he could go back to sleep.

He says, "What are you thinking about?"

"Nothing. You feeling any better?"

He lies back down. He curls up like he's trying to get his entire body around his head. "Hurts, Stephen."

"I know. I know it does."

I can tell by the way he relaxes that I said the right thing.

I crawl back into my bed and look straight up at the ceiling. A minute later, he's snoring, but I don't feel tired anymore.

At least I have Sasha. I think about that and smile a little.

I try to plug me and Sasha into the hospital story. It doesn't work. If this were our story, we would be equal. We'd be taking care of each other and liking each other and everything would be perfect and the same. That's the problem with Marco's story. That there were weird parts about it. Like that the hug hurt, and that they pretend it didn't happen. If it were me and Sasha, it would be perfect.

I should have told a story about us. We should be real.

I should tell her. Tomorrow night.

I hear it loud and hard in my head, like I'm inside a bell. Yes. I should tell her. If there were something wrong with Sasha, I wouldn't mind staying up with her. And it definitely wouldn't be like I'm her brother. Not like how it is with Marco.

I'm not going to get left behind.

BRIAN (AND ALSO JULIA)

Marco jumps on me to wake me up at like 8 a.m. On a Saturday. I should be used to this, because I'm the only one in my whole family who likes sleeping in. But I'm so tired today.

Marco wants to go straight to Julia and tell her about the plan, but as soon as we go downstairs to find her, she answers the phone and tells Marco it's his parents calling from Japan. He sits down in one of the kitchen chairs to talk to them, and he leans over the table and holds his head. He looks so pathetic.

"I'll go talk to Brian," I say.

He nods a little without looking at me.

I squeeze the back of his neck on my way out of the kitchen, and he reaches behind me as soon as I try to walk away. He grabs my wrist, tightly, but only for a second. Then he lets go and says, "Uh-huh, yeah. I'm listening. Sounds perfect."

Seriously, though, his voice. It's like he thinks his parents are off getting tested for some rare disease. They're getting a baby. They're getting his sister. If my mom adopted a kid, I'd think she was a little insane because seriously, seven? But I'd be so totally into it after that. I'd be making her send pictures and brainstorm names with me.

He'll learn. He's acting like a spoiled brat, but every time I try to tell him that, he gets really angry and won't talk to me and I end up apologizing to him, which is so exhausting and frustrating, but I never notice that until later. He'll get over it. His parents have been preparing him for this for a year. But when he actually sees the baby, it'll be different.

I wish I could convince him. But I don't even know what it's like not to have siblings. Marco can live with me and my siblings forever, but there's going to have to be some moment where he sees something he couldn't see before. He's going to need something to click, and I don't think there's anything I can do to help him get there. It's like how Brian is way colorblind, and no matter how many times I explain the difference between red and green, he's not going to get it unless he somehow gets to see it.

"You're all the family I need," he said to me once, months ago, when he was really tired, and I don't know what to make of that.

Anyway, if someone told Brian he would get to see colors, he'd be throwing a party.

Brian is lying on his bed with the door open, reading some book about some kind of science that I probably can't pronounce. He's probably been up for hours. He's so weird.

I stand in the doorway and wave.

He gives me a really tiny smile. It's not mean, it's just so small. "Hey, Stephen."

"Your room is freezing." It always is. The window's open, and it's rainy and cold for June. I don't think Brian feels cold like most people do. He's a robot.

He gets up and digs through his dresser until he finds a sweatshirt. He throws it at me. It's the big fluffy one he wears after swim meets, and it still smells like chlorine. I pull it on and wrap my arms around myself.

I sit down on the foot of the bed and play with the toe of Brian's sock. I'm not even thinking about it while I'm doing it. I just think the bumpy seam feels funny between my fingers.

He says, "What can I do for you, Stephen?"

"Sorry."

He laughs. "I don't know what you're apologizing for."

"Sock. Where have you been lately?"

"Oh. Not anywhere, really. Not doing anything, I mean."

He's the worst liar. My brain shows me a picture, immediately, of exactly where this is going in my case file. Brian's page has practically nothing on it. I could never think of anything to say about him. I guess I don't know him that well.

Anyway, I'm not exactly excited about adding this to his page. Marco always thought it was suspicious that his page is so blank. "Your dad's used to be, too," he said.

"Shut up," I said, and he actually did. But I don't think Marco's ever forgiven Brian for getting too old for us, which is so stupid, and exactly the kind of way an only child thinks.

I look up at Brian and say, "So I do need something, actually."

"I knew it."

I tell him everything about the heist, even though I'm

pretty sure Marco didn't mean for me to reveal the whole thing. To tell the truth, I'm barely listening to myself. I'm using the time I'm speaking to look around Brian's room and look at him. All the little things in here, all of Brian's stuff, feel like souvenirs I brought home from a vacation when I was really little, one I don't remember anymore, but I still have these relics lying around like shipwrecks. My brother's whole room feels like that. Left-over pieces to remember him by.

I wonder how much of this he's taking to college. He can't be planning to take that geode we broke in half on the driveway five years ago, or his Most Improved Swim-mer trophy from when he was seven.

This is stupid. I try to pay attention to what I'm say-ing, but I'm reciting this heist like it's part of my haftorah or something. I'm not even thinking about it.

I try to remember that the only thought I should have about Brian packing is which shirts he's going to leave me to wear when I'm in high school. And then pass down to Marco.

I mean, he's going to come home all the time.

I know that.

I'm still not paying attention to myself, and I pretty much only know I'm done talking when I hear him breathe out really long and slow, the same way Mom does. The same way I do.

Maybe Marco's right, and we do yell all the time. Maybe all we do is yell and breathe out slowly.

Brian reaches his arms out and gives me a hug.

Oh. We do that, too.

"It's nice of you to do this for Marco," he says. "So what's in it for you?"

"Marco's really smart, y'know?" I wait for him to nod. He does. But he's still waiting for an answer.

I say, "So sometimes if I pay enough attention to the way he plans stuff out, I can plan stuff out, too. Once he's gone."

This is the part where Brian should look like he feels sorry for me, but he's still watching me in that same way I can't figure out.

"I'm getting there," I say. "Learning and all that. You should be proud."

Brian doesn't say anything.

I say, "I guess I like playing sidekick."

Brian gives me a lopsided smile. "That's the first time I've heard you put *I guess* in the front of that sentence." When I frown, he goes, "Aw, I'm sorry. Just playing. C'mere," and scoots over so there's room for me to lean against the headboard next to him. We stretch our legs out. The bottoms of my feet barely reach past his knees.

Brian says, "Stevey...you don't think you're maybe getting kind of old for these games?"

"This is a heist. We've never done a heist before."

"It really isn't safe. You're going to be running around by yourselves at night—on prom night, you know? Tons of drunk teenagers driving SUVs and standing up in limos...Does Mom know about this?"

"No. we're telling her we're going to study group I don't even know where she is."

"Saturday morning, so Robbie and Catherine have ballet."

"Right." I pull my knees up and rest my chin on them. He always remembers where we're supposed to be.

"Study group even though school's out?"

"Marco's idea."

"Ah. Of course. You think that's going to work?"

"He said it would." I shove my chin deeper between my kneecaps. "You're not going to help me, are you?"

"Nuh-uh."

"Because you think it's too dangerous. Come on. We're just taking buses."

"You're breaking into the school. And I told you, with Marco, nothing is ever *just*. And maybe he shouldn't be out right now."

"What?"

"Forget it."

"We're not breaking. Just entering."

"You're forging—*trying* to forge—a note from your principal. Do you have any idea the trouble you could get into for that?"

"We don't even go to that school anymore. So it doesn't matter if we get in trouble."

"Yeah, well, newsflash: High school isn't a total starting over."

"It is for Marco."

He breathes out. "Look, Stevey, this is about more than just the risk of this one night. You keep getting yourselves into these situations because they sound like fun, and you end up..."

I wish he'd stop.

He says, "I mean, we know how your last mission worked out, right?"

He's not mad. He never was.

None of them were ever mad at me, and I don't know how to deal with that.

And suddenly I'm seeing Dad all over the stupid room. There's this baseball cap on the floor that I don't think I've ever seen Brian wear, but I can see Dad in it without even closing my eyes. There's a tie on a hook that he probably borrowed from Dad. There's a picture of everyone Sherri-aged or older at Brian's Bar Mitzvah, Dad's hand tight on Bri's shoulder. Actually, that one feels like someone planted it here just to make me mad.

"Yeah," I mumble.

His pocket buzzes, and he takes his phone out and checks it. "I've got to take this, kid."

So I have to leave? "Jessica?"

"Or something." He stands up and pulls on a pair of boots. "Listen. I want you to promise you're not going to go through with this, okay? Don't make me have to be the tattletale who goes to Mom, okay?"

"So don't go to Mom."

"Stephen, come on. Be compassionate. She doesn't need this to worry about."

I don't say that this mission feels like the most compassionate thing I've ever done.

He wouldn't get it.

"Promise," Brian says.

"Okay. God."

He nods at me and he's gone. I've never lied to Brian before. But for some reason I don't feel bad about it today.

It's not like he's been entirely open with me lately, right? Especially if that phone call really isn't from Jessica. Who is he talking to? Where is he going?

Marco would want to investigate this, that's for sure. But we don't have time for that, and...okay, maybe I don't really want to know. Maybe I've uncovered enough secrets in my family for one year, you know? I just want everything to be normal and okay for a little while. And if that means I have to pretend not to see weird things when I see them, pretend I'm not as good a detective as I am...well, so be it.

I just need to stop Marco from picking up the trail, because I know he won't see it that way. And anyway, let's be honest, way bigger fish and all that.

I go back to my room. Marco's still on the phone, so I lie on the bed with the detective notebook and practice Brian's handwriting.

"Hey."

I look up at Julia in the doorway. "Hey."

"Your plan is stupid."

"Yeah."

"I'm going to text around and see if I can find out what teachers are going to be there, I guess. It's not like it's going to be hard."

"Thanks."

She shrugs a little. "I probably owe you one for something." She smiles a little. "And Marco's so excited about it."

"You feeling better today?"

"So anyway, yeah. I'll text people."

I chew on my lip. "Okay."

She leaves, and I feel stupid and deflated, partly because my sister's sad, but also because Marco managed to convince my heartbroken sister to help us, and I couldn't convince my has-everything-he-could-ever-want big brother to write on a piece of stationery.

I hear my mom and my siblings get home and start thundering around the kitchen and the living room, but I stay where I am and keep practicing Brian's handwriting. I need it to be perfect. I need Marco not to know that I've already screwed up and things are already getting messy.

MARCO PLAYS SUPERHERO AND SASHA HAS ULTERIOR MOTIVES

Luke is waiting at the basketball courts just like Marco said he would be. He's by himself, and he stands there with his hands in his pockets and watches us the whole walk from the bike rack to the field and the basketball courts.

"Creepy," I say.

"He's just standing there." Marco fishes the iPod out of his pocket. "He's not doing anything wrong. Fifty dollars. Here I go."

I can see Sasha to our right, out by the field. She's standing on the sidelines next to the coaches cheering for kids around Catherine's age. "Come on, you can run faster than that! Come on, Maddy!" Her curly hair is back in a ponytail that's bouncing over her shoulder.

"Put your eyes back in your face," Marco says.

I say, "Why are all kindergarteners named Maddy?"

"Yeah, because that's what you're thinking about."

"Are you going to shut up and do the iPod? Or do I need to do it for you?"

The easiest way to get Marco to do something is to imply that he's not absolutely the best man for the job. He tosses the iPod into the air and snatches it back. "You wish. Time me. I'll be done in seconds."

"We'll race."

"Nah, not you." He gives my cheek a smack. "You go spend time with your girlfriend."

For every single soccer-playing five-year-old who might have just heard that, one of my organs shriveled and died. "She's not my—"

"Just *go*. God. I'm going to make Luke throw in an extra ten, watch me. Watch me. Except watch your girlfriend, really." He messes up his hair and heads over to Luke. Luke's been watching us this whole time, but he nods when Marco gets close like he's just seeing him. Marco is slouching. He doesn't try to make himself look taller.

Sasha's finishing a huddle with the kids, and she cheers for them on their way out to do another drill. She climbs up the bleachers a little to grab a water bottle, and that's when she sees me.

And smiles.

"Hey!" she calls. She turns and says something to the coach, who nods. Then she runs over to me. "What are you doing here?"

I shrug. "Marco."

She looks over by the basketball courts. "Oh." She shoves her tongue against the gap between her front teeth. She does that all the time. It's in her character profile, which isn't nearly as detailed as Benji's. It should be.

"We don't need as much on Sasha," Marco told me, ages ago. "It's not like we're going to forget. Not like Benji. He's new." And I never argued, I guess.

Sasha and Marco and I used to all be best friends back when we were really little. Then she started playing basketball and lacrosse and doing karate and going to tap dancing lessons and being really busy all the time, and Marco and I just wanted to play detective and try to follow Brian around. At the time, her skipping out on us to go to practice all the time was this really massive deal, so we sort of accidentally stopped being friends and tried not to look at each other in the hallway. If anyone asked me, I said I hated Sasha, but I could never think of a good excuse for why. If they asked Marco, he'd shrug and say something like, "That file is sealed" or "That information is classified." I don't know what Sasha said. I still feel bad about saying I hated her.

Then last year, Marco pointed out that I was looking at her all the time. I didn't even mean to. I'd just be sitting in class and looking at her. And I didn't feel anything, not then, so it was so *weird* that I was looking at her, because I never thought about why I was doing it.

I'd never really... thought about girls before that. They'd just been kind of there. I guess I thought they were on ice or something, waiting for me to get old enough to want them. Staying frozen until I was ready to turn into Brian and start obsessing over whether or not to call them or wait for them to call.

At the beginning of this year, Sasha and I got paired together on a project about the ozone layer, and she showed up to school on the day of our report wearing this costume she made out of blue fabric draped all over her with a big black spot painted in the middle. She was supposed to be the sky, but with a hole in it. She wore it all day and smiled at people who laughed at her.

That was when I started feeling things.

So whenever I feel like Marco's reasons for liking Benji are stupid, I remind myself that I'm in love with a girl because she dressed up like the sky with a hole in it.

She says, "Why do you keep looking over at them?"

Guh. I say, "I don't know. He's weird with Luke. It's like he has this whole different personality just for Luke."

He listens to Luke.

Sasha says, "Does he like Luke, do you think?"

"What? No!"

I look at Marco. Luke's saying something without looking at him, and Marco's scuffing his sneaker against the ground in that shy way.

Ohhhh God.

What if he does?

I say, "Marco likes Benji. Everyone knows that."

"He can like both."

I watch Luke and Marco. Luke is telling Marco something. His arms are crossed and he's smiling in a way that isn't friendly at all.

I say, "Luke is kind of horrible to him."

She raises an eyebrow.

"You're thinking about the locker thing."

"I guess I don't know who else would have done it."

"Does Marco think Luke's behind it?"

"Marco hasn't said anything about any of it." Honestly, I don't think he'd believe it's Luke, either. He wouldn't believe it's someone he talks to all the time. He doesn't think people would do that. That's why he'll avoid the issue altogether. Marco can be really stupid about some things. I don't think he even knows that Luke's horrible to him.

Sasha says, "So it seems like we have a mystery on our hands, huh?" She has her arms crossed, just like Luke, and she's smiling and laughing a little. She is trying to suck me in and it is working.

"I guess so," I say.

It's totally not a mystery.

But God, I miss mysteries.

"You should find proof. You're the big detective." I can't tell if she's teasing me or not. "I tried to talk to Dr. Slade about the hate crimes yesterday, but he kept saying he couldn't discuss it. How am I supposed to be a lawyer someday if no one will tell me what's going on? How am I going to be high school freaking president if I'm not informed?"

She's good at giving speeches, clearly.

I mean, I'd vote for her.

Yeah, shut up.

She says, "Did you see the paper this morning?"

I shake my head. Sasha reads the paper every day. It's in her profile. I've never read anything but comics and sometimes sports, but I like that she always thinks there's this chance I might have read it that day. Someday I'm going to read it. She'll ask and I'll say yes and recite a headline to her. She'll love that.

She said, "Usual stuff, reports on violence like it's a new thing. But they mentioned hate crimes in schools around here. Just this really quick mention of it, and they didn't say that it was here, but you could totally tell. The details lined up. And it's going on in other schools. It's worse at Taft."

"Yeah?"

"Maybe they're connected."

Or maybe they're not. I'm never good at keeping that in mind. Marco tries to drill it into my head all the time. "We are not Occam and this is not a razor," he says, which means basically that sometimes the un-simplest answer is the easiest answer, and the easiest answer is the right answer. Just because things are always connected in movies doesn't mean they are in real life. Sometimes things just happen at the same time.

Happened with Dad, anyway.

"Marco's going to private school," I say. "Luke won't be able to do anything to him."

"You're really convinced it's Luke, aren't you?"

"I guess." Yeah. I'm trying to concentrate on Sasha, but I can't stop glancing over, like I'm expecting Luke to hit Marco. He never has before, even after Marco punched him that time.

"Whoever it is," Sasha says. "Even if Marco's safe, there are, you know, tons of kids like Marco."

I hear phrases like that a lot. Kids like Marco. Everyone says it when they don't want to say *gay*.

"You care about things," she says. "That's one of the reasons I'm talking to you."

I swallow. "What's the other reason?"

If this were a movie, at this point she'd take another sip of water, glance back to make sure her kids are busy, and then kiss me.

She takes a drink of water.

"You're a detective," she says.

I guess that's okay, too.

She says, "No one's going to listen to us if we don't have proof. We need to catch LukeDarthVaderwhoever in the act. We need to know who was free at the time of the crimes. We need to know other stuff the suspect has done. Harassing Marco. Or leading him on. Or, you know. Throwing snow cones."

"Heh." Most of the time when I'm talking to Sasha, I feel like I can only use words that are one syllable long. Apparently right now I can only make little sounds like some kind of sick sheep.

"So, do you have anything good on Luke already? In your case file or whatever?"

"I thought you thought that was stupid." *Stupid.* That's two syllables. Good job, Stephen.

She laughs. "It's only stupid when there isn't a real mystery. The case of the broken bookshelf. The case of Benji's runny nose."

She's exaggerating. Mostly. Okay, so maybe Marco was *really* worried about Benji when he was sick. But we're detectives. It's what we do. We might have squelched an epidemic with our emergency anonymous delivery of orange juice and a get-well-soon card to his front door.

I say, "The thing is, I'm already on a mission."

She raises an eyebrow. "Yeah?"

I nod.

"Is it as important as mine?"

I know what Marco would want me to say.

But.

Well.

Sasha.

I say, "No."

She nods in this very smart, sympathetic way. It's pretty.

"But we still need your help," I say.

Then she smiles.

I drop my voice down and tell Sasha our plan. I try to mention Benji as little as possible, but it's not like I can leave him out completely. She raises her eyebrows all skeptical the first time I say his name, but after that she shrugs and listens. "That is so Marco," she says when I'm done.

"Right?"

"And it's so like you to tag along."

"So you'll help us?"

She chews on her lip. "I guess it would give us an answer either way. As long as you're there to protect him. In case Benji . . . doesn't take it well."

"Um, of course, yeah."

"All I have to do is grab the stationery, right?" she says.

"Yeah."

"That's kind of . . . lame."

"You want to do more?"

She takes a sip of her water. "Yeah, absolutely. Like the old days, right? I always got to be that girl in the corner with the trench coat and the fedora, passing out folders full of hidden information." When we played detective when we were really little, Sasha always had the best ideas, so she got to make up the cases and we had to try to figure them out. That was really great, actually, because then everything always had an answer and was always fair.

I say, "The thing is, we don't really need a lot of hidden information for this one. Just the stationery. It's a pretty straightforward plan."

She thinks about this for a long time, looking back toward the field for a while. The sun is shadowing her face into two different colors. Her eyes and lips are dark, and then the light hits her hair and makes it look charged with electricity.

Then she says, "So how about if we make it a little less straightforward."

I really shouldn't say, "I'm listening," but I do.

"You want the stationery." She smiles. "I want something in return."

This would be another good place for us to kiss.

Nope.

"Okay…" I say.

"I need a sidekick, too. I want to save the world or whatever, get myself some good karma." She nods toward her soccer playing kids. "Be a good role model."

"Maybe get something on your transcript?"

"Yeah, no one's perfect. So help me out here. Put some serious time into looking up the hate crimes. And I'll do the same. We'll grab some evidence and motive and means, et cetera. And we meet up at some point tonight and compare notes."

"Does it have to be tonight?" I can't believe I'm saying this. I should be dying to be with Sasha whenever. I shouldn't be annoyed, but I kind of am. "I don't really have any serious time I can give to the investigation."

She says, "Are you kidding? Tonight's perfect. You're going to be all over town. You have a great chance of seeing something, or of noticing if Marco's hiding anything."

"Marco's not—"

"And if someone comes looking for him, you'll be right there. And you have to be. Everything's crazy, cops are busy with drunk teenagers… no one's going to be looking out for Marco but us."

"Marco's not in any real danger," I say.

Because that's just the truth, okay? It has to be.

Luke shoves Marco by the shoulder a little, like they're playing around. Marco doesn't look up.

I guess catching the bad guy and clearing the name of the guy he loves really would make this all the more romantic for Marco, right? He'd understand that.

Yeah. He'd understand that.

Sasha says, "We'll meet up here later? I'll bring the stationery. That's how I'll make sure you come back." She grins. "I'll also raid the office the best I can and bring you everything I can find that might help us figure this out. And we'll work on it together, okay? All you have to do is keep an eye out for anything suspicious, do a background check or two, and figure out if Marco knows anything more, and the rest of your time you devote to your thing with Marco. It's just two missions. You can handle that, right?"

"Of course. Of course I can handle it."

But then she says, "So . . . Stephen? Maybe, while you're doing your mission, both missions . . . maybe concentrate on playing bodyguard a little, too. I'm just saying. Compared to the stuff in the paper, locker kicking is pretty tame. So, just, you know."

"No one's going to hurt him."

She nods a little. "I know." She looks up. "I think it's going to rain soon."

"Marco!" I call. Luke mouths something that looks a lot like *polo*. Marco says a few more words to Luke and runs over to me.

"Hey." He's kind of out of breath.

"How'd it go?" I say.

"Mission accomplished. Hey, Sasha. My assistant filled you in?"

"He did."

"Well?" he says.

We look at him.

He says, "Where's the stationery? We're not leaving without it. And we're on a tight schedule. We have a beautiful lady to meet next. Named Julia."

Sasha looks like she's about to make some joke, but then Luke walks by and gives Marco this kind of rough pat on the shoulder on his way by. It makes him stumble. Marco doesn't say anything, and Luke doesn't look at me and Sasha until she clears her throat and says, "Hi to you, too."

"What do you want?" he says to her.

"Not you."

He rolls his eyes and walks away, calling, "Have fun on your little mission, Marco!"

Sasha lowers her shoulders.

That's when I notice that Marco has edged a little closer to me.

"You okay?" I say.

Marco pulls away hard and gives me a look. "Yeah, Stephen, God. Are *you* okay? Geez." I don't know what he's talking about, and I don't think he does, either.

Sasha clears her throat and says, "I'll grab the stationery." She jogs up to the building.

Marco and I don't say anything for a minute.

I say, "So everything went okay?"

"Yeah. I'm a superhero."

It's weird that he isn't gloating, though, about how he overcharged Luke, or about how funny it is that he's going to accidentally listen to *The Sound of Music* again and again.

Then he smiles. "I knew it would work."

"Yeah."

I'm a good detective. But he's better. And that means that even though I know he's hiding something, I'm not going to get to know what it is until he decides to give it up.

He better decide to give it up before I meet with Sasha. I'm not letting her down.

I say, "You sure everything's okay?" and he says, "Leave me alone, okay?"

Fine.

Sasha comes back with an envelope and hands it to me. Marco hugs her, and I definitely don't, and while we're walking around the building to find Julia, I peek inside the envelope. Plain printer paper, and a note that says *8 p.m. Outside the gym. Then you'll get your stationery. Trust no one. Keep him safe.*

The girl is good.

AND HERE THERE ARE COMPLICATIONS

We're halfway around the building when it starts raining. All of a sudden. Hard.

Marco and I curse and duck under the overhang around the edge of the building. Through the rain, I can barely see that there's someone twenty feet away, by the front door, until she opens up a huge red umbrella. We jog up, and Julia lets us under.

"Robbie has a fever," she says.

"Guh."

"Essentially. Brian's driving him around because he won't stop crying. Probably another ear infection. So don't you two get sick. Big heist and all that."

"I never get sick," Marco says. Yeah, he gets sick all the time.

I can still barely recognize that this is Julia. She has on sunglasses, a trench coat, and big floppy hat. She's holding a manila folder. She looks like the girl Sasha is trying to be.

Sasha runs by just then. She gives us a quick wave, but she's trying to keep the kids as dry as possible while she runs them to their parents' cars.

"What's with the sunglasses?" Marco says.

"I didn't want anyone to recognize me hanging out by the middle school."

I've never heard her say anything like that before. "Julia?"

She groans and takes the sunglasses up. Her eyes are puffy and pink. "It's just been a long day, okay?"

I give her a hug before Marco can. He grabs her the minute I let go.

"Thanks, guys." She laughs, just a little. "Really, I'm fine." She sniffles and looks out at the rain.

The only thing I can think of to say is *you're not fine,* and that isn't going to help anything.

She says, "It's so stupid, you know? All of my friends think I'm acting like an idiot. Except they won't say that, 'cause they're all afraid of me. They're all just…"

I've seen this since I was in sixth grade and she was in eighth. All her friends are these girls who work so hard to be pretty that they all end up looking the same. Their hair is freaky straight and hangs off their head in panels like siding on a house. They draw these really skinny black lines around their eyes that make them look distorted and sick. Julia doesn't do any of that. The girls find her anyway.

And she's too nice to tell them she doesn't want to be their queen.

Or not smart enough to find another way out.

I hate that it might be true.

She says, "Anyway." She shakes her head a little and pulls a manila folder out of her purse. "Okay, this is everything I found. Everyone knows Ms. Tannelbaum is going to be there, and a little more digging told me Mr. Sikes. There's got to be more than the two of them, but this is all I could find."

Marco looks through the folder. "You got all that, Stephen?"

I jot this all down in the notebook. "Yep."

Julia says, "Your best bet is going to be playing Mr. Sikes. It's mean, but it's almost foolproof, and you can make it kind of harmless. He has a twelve-year-old kid—he's in private school—and he had an older son, Brian's age, who died in a car crash last year."

Marco puts the pieces together the fastest, like always. "Tell Mr. Sikes we have to get in because we really need to see Stephen's older brother, please please please we love him so much."

"Essentially."

I say, "That's . . . really mean."

Marco says, "Not *really*. It's not like we're using it for nefarious purposes. This is an honorable mission, Stevey."

"But it has nothing to do with Brian."

"So you give him a hug while we're in there. Whatever."

Julia says, "If you decide not to use that, try to think of something involving the safety of a cat. Miss Tannelbaum has eight cats." She checks her phone. "Brian says he can swing by and pick me up. You guys should get lost by then."

"Yeah."

Marco looks at me. "What?"

She says, "If he finds out you're doing this . . . I don't even know. You guys have to be careful. Who knows how much of tonight he's going to be driving around with the baby. Be on the lookout, all right?"

I say, "Brian's going to be at prom. How much time does he really have to drive Robbie in circles?"

Julia says, "Actually—"

Marco says, "No, no, wait. Brian knows about this. It doesn't matter if he sees us. He's supposed to see us. He's part of the plan. He knows all about this."

She says, "He knows that Stephen said he wouldn't do it, yeah."

"What?"

I breathe out. "It's fine. Everything's fine. I've been practicing my fancy handwriting. I can write the note just as well as Brian could."

"You told me everything was worked out."

"It *is* worked out, did you not just hear me?"

Julia's still focused on her phone. "Great. Now Robbie's throwing up. Poor kid..."

Marco says, "I can't believe this, Stephen."

I look at Julia. "Is he okay?"

"Pay attention to me!" Marco says.

"Are you kidding me right now, Marco? Seriously? Am I ever *not* paying attention to you? Is there ever a single second *ever* where you don't force me to pay attention to you?"

Now Julia looks up. She chews on her cheek and looks between the two of us, slowly.

"You guys okay?" she says. She sounds like a teacher,

when they catch you talking in class and they go, "Are you finished?" There's only one answer. You don't get to think about it first.

"Yeah," we mumble.

I exhale long and slow.

Marco swallows. "Fine." He hands the folder to me. "Check this off on our list, please, Stephen. Julia has been lovely and helpful. And while we're on the bus on the way to the prom, you will do a perfect imitation of your brother's adult handwriting and tell a very sad story about Brian and something with cats. Something that will get us in."

"Yeah."

If I tell Marco that I don't have the stationery yet, he might actually strangle me right here.

Besides. I'll have it by then. We'll be back here just before eight for our bus transfer anyway. If I can get Marco distracted for just a minute, I can get Sasha to slip me the stationery.

Except I have to have information on the hate crimes by then, or there's no way she'll give me anything. And then I have to write the note before we get to the prom, which would be fine except Marco's going to be freaking out about why I haven't written it already, and I have no idea what I'm going to write.

Not to mention that if Marco finds out I have another case going on, he'll lose his mind. He's clearly uninterested in stopping the hate crimes. And God forbid I have anything on my mind besides getting the guy.

How did this get so complicated before it even started?

Marco says, "Stephen, go look over our new documents. Over there." He points somewhere. Vaguely. The point is, obviously, look over them *not here*.

I'm about to ask why, but then I realize I don't really care. "Yeah, fine."

"What's going on?" Julia says.

I walk away, staying under the overhang. But instead of looking at the folders, I take out my phone and text Sherri.

> need you to find out everything you can
> about the hate crimes. & facebook stalk
> luke gorman.

Sherri knows more about computers than anyone in my grade. And probably in Brian's grade.

> its horrible here. sick baby

She doesn't know much about grammar, though.

yeah. sorry. you'll help me out?

yeah

Cool.

I could ask her to stalk Benji, but it seems stupid because there's nothing on Benji's page that Marco hasn't seen. He's gone through it pixel by pixel a million times. It's mostly pictures of him with his brothers and with bands.

And with girls. Never doing anything but hugging them, but...

A lot, a lot of pictures of him with girls.

I am watching my best friend march right into heartbreak, I'm pretty sure.

I give the documents a quick glance, but then I look up to see what Marco and Julia are doing. He's talking to her, his hands stuffed in his pockets, not looking at her, and after a minute she nods and takes out her purse.

She opens her wallet and hands him a few bills. He hugs her hard and kisses her cheek.

Julia's giving him money?

My head goes *click*. Because Marco needs money. Because Luke didn't pay him.

Why would Marco let Luke take it and not pay?

I swallow as Marco jogs toward me. He's clearly still kind of mad at me, and despite the new revelation that Luke pushed him around, I'm not totally pleased with him, either, but I say, "Thanks for taking care of her."

Marco looks surprised. "I've got your back, you know that."

"I've got yours."

Marco gives me this strange, sad little smile. "Sure."

IT'S JUST THAT HE'S KINDA SMALL

First section of plan completed successfully. Mother has not been in contact and therefore has likely not discovered the fake study group. Baby, sick, must have distracted her.

Bikes successfully stashed in locker room [girls'], 5:50 bus successfully boarded. Bus was exactly two minutes late, which so far has caused us no problems.

Each of us holds $100. We are armed with our camera and our case file. We are ready to rent tuxedos, and also to overcome any and all possible complications.

Will be meeting Sasha at the school when we drop off
our street clothes and change buses to obtain (a)
stationery and (b) evidence in the hate crime case.
Hopefully, I can complete the transaction without Marco
noticing.

Hopefully, part of this transaction will involve me telling
her I like her. And her saying she likes me, too.

Hopefully, Marco won't see this page of the file.

At least it's stopped raining.

Marco slams both his hands down on the counter. "You have to have *something* here."

Nic has his feet up on the counter and a magazine open on his lap. Behind him, there's nothing but one rack of jackets, some fraying and stripped of buttons and some just brown and very sad.

He barely looks up from the magazine.

"It's prom night, kid. We've had kids in here all day, kids who already had tuxes reserved. You've got to make arrangements ahead of time."

"It's an emergency," I say. "See, my dad just died? And

they just moved the funeral up to tonight. And we don't have anything to wear."

Nic still doesn't raise his head. "You want to wear a tux to a funeral? Try again, kid."

I should really leave the lying to Marco.

Marco puts his arm around my shoulders and pulls me in. I feel like a dog on a leash. Marco says, "He gets a little crazy when he's desperate. Look. You've got to have something. Two tuxes. Just two. Can you check the back or something?"

Nic finally stands up and studies Marco. He says, "I'm sorry, I don't think—"

"It *is* an emergency," Marco says. "It's not a funeral. It's so much hugely more huge than a funeral. This is a matter of heart or no heart. If we don't get tuxedos tonight, a boy is going to get on a plane to England for three months with *no* idea that someone thinks he is the best part of the world. Do you want to be responsible for that kind of human misery? Isn't the world cold enough already?"

Nic says, "The issue isn't—"

"Because seriously, there is so much bad stuff going on. It's like a whole world full of bad stuff. There are so few things about the world that are at all okay right now. I can really count them on two fingers, and one of them is this kid right here next to me, and he needs a tux. And everything else is just so very bad, and that's what I'm feeling right now. And what I want to be feeling is a tux. On my body. So that I can go and I can make one tiny thing right for this guy who is getting on a plane to England and maybe somehow that will make less bad stuff for everyone."

Marco.

He reaches his hand into his pocket and holds out our money. His emergency money. My money. Julia's money. All of it. "A hundred dollars a tux. One night. Look." He spreads the bills out on the counter like he's about to play solitaire. "Two hundred dollars. It's right there. You can have all of it."

I say, "Marco, the cab."

"Shut up. We'll make it work."

Yeah, of course, when he wants to go off-book, then we can make it work. I thought he didn't do Plan Bs.

Nic is thinking. Marco stands absolutely still.

I've only seen one person say no to Marco, ever. It was his mom, just this one time. It was something stupid. I think it was whether he could have a soda while we were at a restaurant or something, which is totally dumb because he knows he can't because if he has any caffeine at all he gets a migraine for like twenty years. And he never gets angsty about that, except this one time when I guess he thought he could get his way, I don't know, and she just said "No," no discussion, and Marco looked completely confused. He can usually talk them into anything, eventually. He knows the right things to say. It didn't work that time, and he didn't talk for like half an hour after. And it wasn't even like he was pouting as much as he was kind of freaked out by the whole thing. He has this way of only saying things that people will say yes to, and I don't know if that's because he asks the right questions or because he has that face that makes you want to give him all the cookies from your lunch box.

Anyway, I've been wondering ever since how Mrs. Kimura did it, because I think eventually Marco wears everybody down. He's just *relentless*. If Benji says no to him, honestly, he'll deserve a medal.

Except, you know, no he won't.

Nic takes the money and counts it out, even though he just saw Marco do it. Then he hands it back to Marco and says, "All right. Let's see what we can do."

In five minutes, three guys who appeared out of nowhere have stretched us, squished us, pinched us, buttoned us, and thrown us into dressing rooms to try on piece after piece after piece. For a store that supposedly didn't have any tuxes left, they're finding a million things to fasten onto my body. I don't even know what half these things are. One of the guys has to come into the dressing room and show me where exactly a cummerbund is supposed to go, and even after he puts it on me, I still don't think I know what just happened.

But after it's all done, I look at myself in the mirror in the dressing room and realize that I don't have the Robbie curse anymore. I don't look like a baby when I'm dressed up.

I think this is the first time I've worn a suit that really fits. The last time I wore one was to Brian's Bar Mitzvah, and it was his hand-me-down. The jacket was so huge that I looked like a big square with tiny little legs underneath. I never bought the suit for my Bar Mitzvah. It's like somehow we knew it wasn't going to happen.

But this tuxedo, this fits. I never knew my shoulders and my chest were wider than my waist. I look like an adult. Like Brian. Mom says I look like Brian, but I've never seen it before. That's why I couldn't borrow his student ID. Brian looks so much like Dad.

Maybe I should wear a tux every day. People would take me seriously.

I say, "Hey, Marco!" and step outside the dressing room. He's already out, chewing on his lip.

He's swimming in a jacket three times his size, and his pants are dripping off his waist. Even his shoes look too big. It's like he shrunk and his clothes didn't change size with him. Except Marco was always this small, and I guess that's the problem.

He looks like Robbie.

He looks at Nic in disgust. "Come on," he says. "You have to have something better than this."

Nic says, "I don't think we have anything small enough. We don't have a lot of kid-sized ones, and they're all rented out. June weddings and stuff."

Marco's cheeks are bright red. "Come on."

"I'm sorry."

Marco swallows, but then he turns and looks at me and his face changes. "Wow. Oh, man, Stevey, look at you."

"Yeah?"

"You look like a prince or something."

"Thanks. So what are we going to do about you?"

Marco opens the dressing room and stands in the doorway, looking at himself in the mirror. He swings his upper body back and forth, so the sleeves hanging off his hands flap around like he's some kind of flightless bird.

"Well," he says thoughtfully. "I can't wear this."

"Probably not."

He sighs. "I have the suit at home that I got for your Bar Mitzvah."

"Perfect."

He rubs his forehead. "Going to my house wasn't part of the plan."

"We have enough time." I go over and squeeze his shoulder. Even my hand looks older now. I wish I had one of those big silver watches. "It'll be okay."

He looks up at me and smiles a little. "Thanks, Stevey."

I take my old clothes out of my backpack to change again, and Nic raises his eyebrows. "You're going to stuff the tux in there?"

That was the plan. I look at him.

Nic shakes his head. "It'll get all wrinkled. You can't do that."

I look at Marco. He says, "You'll have to wear it."

"I'm running around in a tux? While you're wearing jeans?"

"I'll change into the suit as soon as I'm home," he says. "Solidarity." He takes my hundred dollars and heads to the register. "Until then, we'll pretend you're my butler."

I can't believe I'm saying this, but for a minute I thought he was going to say *my date*, which would be gross but would at least be better than butler.

I AM RELATED TO A CRIMINAL MASTERMIND

We figure out what bus to take to Marco's house, but it's not until we've walked the twenty minutes from the bus stop that we realize we don't have a key.

We used to be so much better at this stuff. What happened to our detective skills?

"We're too old," Marco says. He's reading my mind again.

"Don't say that."

"We act like little kids when we play detective, y'know?"

"And now we're all big and grown up." I definitely say this sarcastically, but Marco nods in this way that makes it obvious that he didn't catch it. Or maybe he's ignoring it on purpose.

"It's going to be fine, you know?" he says.

"We'll get in somehow, yeah."

"Next year. I meant next year."

I don't say anything.

"I mean it," he says. "You're going to be fine. I know you will."

Except he doesn't know it, and isn't that kind of the point? He'll have no way of knowing. I don't say anything.

He looks down at his hoodie and sneakers. "I seriously need a suit. I can't believe you're going to be in a tux and I'm in a suit."

"No one will notice." I don't even know the difference between a tux and a suit, really.

Marco says, "Trust me, if Benji's really into guys, he'll notice," and he laughs in this way that sounds kind of cold, or at least lonely.

I give him a boost up to his bedroom window, and he stands on my hands and starts fussing with the screen. "Hope I don't get you dirty," he says, and there's a bit of an edge in his voice. "In your nice clothes."

"Hey."

"What?"

"Don't be a jerk. Jerkweasel."

He grumbles to himself for a minute, then says, "Sorry. Once I look good, too, it'll be okay."

"Gee, thanks."

"Now *hey* back at you." He turns around as much as he can and looks at me. "Look, sorry if this makes me a jerk, but you're not the one who needs to look good tonight."

"Then why am I even coming?"

"Why do you do this? I say one thing and it turns into this huge deal. I'm not saying I didn't want you here. I'm saying you don't have to make someone fall in love with you tonight. That's it. I want you here. Okay?"

I nod a little.

Although he's not exactly right. Wow, Sasha's going to see me in this tux. I'll get off the bus and walk up to the school and sweep her off her feet or something. I'm like James Bond right now.

But if he's forgotten I ever thought about telling Sasha, I'm not going to remind him. Let him think the night's all about him. Let him be surprised for once.

Marco starts tugging on the screen, but it doesn't budge. I give him a few minutes even after we've both figured out that it's not going to work. I guess neither of us wants to talk right now.

Eventually I let him down and take a picture of the locked window. "Let's try the back door," he says.

We don't have any more luck here. Marco breaks off a skinny tree branch and tries to wiggle it into the keyhole. I don't know how he thinks this is going to work, but he squeezes his eyebrows together and jams his tongue against his teeth. It takes me way too long to figure out that he's frustrated, not concentrating.

He throws the branch on the ground and curses in Italian. "What kind of parents don't leave their kid a spare key? *God.* They're *trying* to make my life an unliveable place."

"They left one with my mom. I could call her…"

"No." He points at me. "Don't you dare."

"Do you want to get in the house or not?"

"Not like that. No way." He paces in tight circles.

I take out my cell phone. "Then we don't have any choice," I say. "I'm calling a locksmith."

He's giving me that look again, like I'm too stupid for him to even tolerate.

"My demon little sister," I say. Catherine can break into anything. Between that and the sock stealing, she's definitely going to be the heir to my master thief throne. Kid's a beast. My family's the only one in the world that's allowed to lock doors during Hide and Seek, because we always make Catherine be It. And she loves it. "Okay, technically I'm calling Julia and telling her to bring my demon little sister."

"No." He tries to snatch the phone from me, but I'm holding it up too high. "Come on, Stephen, *don't.*"

"What is your problem?"

"This is supposed to be just us."

I breathe out long and slow, then I dial Julia. He kicks the ground and crosses his arms over his chest.

"How am I supposed to get there?" Julia says, after I've explained the situation. "It's not like Catherine can bike all that way."

"Can Mom bring you?"

"Stephen!" Marco whispers.

I wave my hand to shut him up.

Julia says, "Busy with Robbie."

"Then Brian's home."

"No, he dropped him off and left right after."

"Where is he all the time?" I say. "With Jessica?" Or last minute prom stuff, I guess.

She laughs. "Nice work, detective. They broke up last week."

Oh, man. I sit down on one of Marco's deck chairs. "Are you kidding me?" I say. Brian and Jessica have been together since I was in elementary school.

I can't believe this.

Is he even okay?

"She dumped him good," Julia says. "I can't believe you didn't know this."

"How do *you* know? I don't think anyone else does."

Marco finally looks up from the ground, "Did we miss a clue?" he says.

Of course that's what he cares about. He doesn't even know what the mystery is, and he's wondering if we've maybe missed a clue for something.

"I heard him on the phone with someone last night," Julia says. "He was trying to be quiet, but I heard him say something about how she totally broke his heart. It was...really sad, actually. But his voice was weird. Like he was telling someone a secret. He definitely didn't want anyone to hear him. And it was weird and late."

"There's something going on with him," I say. Before I can stop myself.

Marco's getting more excited by the minute. He bounces a little and goes, "Who are our suspects?" He grabs the notebook out of my backpack.

Julia says, "What do you mean?"

I take a deep breath. "Nothing," I say. "He's just been gone a lot."

"You know," Julia says, "it's his age." She sounds like Mom.

"Yeah."

"I'll get Mom to let me take Catherine for a walk," she says. "I need to get out of the house anyway. We'll get on a bus."

"Thanks."

"You're lucky it's not raining anymore, or you'd be out of luck," she says. "There are limits to my charity." She hangs up.

My heart's beating in that fast but final way, like after you're done running a mile. There's something comforting about it, because each crazy beat reminds you that you're calming down.

Then I see Marco's face.

And he isn't calm at all.

He says, "What's up with your brother?"

"Nothing."

"It sounds like a mystery."

"No, it's not."

"But—"

"We're not even supposed to have any other missions tonight, and this isn't...he's upset, Marco. This isn't fun."

Marco's quiet for a minute, then he says, "Okay. I'm sorry."

I'm not sure he's ever actually apologized to me before. Ever.

"Anyway, it doesn't matter." He sits down in a chair a few feet away from me. "We shouldn't have other missions tonight, because we already have this one, and this one is already failed because we're not getting into the house so everything's ruined so we should just turn in our badges right now."

"You're driving me insane."

"Yeah."

Julia and Catherine show up pretty quickly. Julia's hair is up in a high ponytail, and I can tell by Catherine's hair that she made Julia try the same thing on her, but Julia did a horrible job. I pull Catherine over to me and fix it. Marco's judging so hard, but you don't get to be the older brother of two girls without figuring out how to do a ponytail. Julia's too clumsy. I have to do hair all the time. It's okay.

Julia says, "Wow, Stephen, look at you."

"He looks really nice," Marco says, softly.

"Tell me about it," she says. "And they tell me *I'm* the pretty one."

"Pretty," Catherine says, and she kisses my cheek.

I smack Julia, but Marco chews on his knuckle and says, his eyes still down, "I'd kill to look like either of you."

Catherine reaches out her hand to him, and he takes it, after a minute, and with a look on his face like he thinks it might be a trap. But at least he takes it.

"Okay, Kitty Cat," Julia says. "Here's your target."

"Help me?" she says.

Julia frowns a little, then she kneels down next to Catherine. "Yeah, I'll help you. You nervous?"

I say, "What's up?"

"She doesn't want to mess up," Julia says. She leans into Catherine's ear and whispers to her for a minute, and then Catherine grins and smiles and says she's ready.

Julia stands up and gets her wallet, and Marco says, "What'd you say?"

She shrugs a little. "I just made her feel better," she says, like it's the easiest thing in the world. That's the thing about Julia. She can't handle ponytails, but she can handle our worries like no one I've ever met.

I guess that's why Marco told her . . . whatever he told her that made her give him the money. He trusts her.

Julia hands Catherine her library card, and Catherine gets to work sliding it between the door and the frame.

Marco, to his credit, doesn't rush her or mumble to himself. He gives her a smile and echoes the encouraging things we say, and the rest of the time he hangs back quietly. He doesn't even give me any dirty looks or mutter about how we're letting them invade our heist, or that this wasn't part of the plan. He looks smaller than usual, if that's possible, with his hands stuffed in his pockets and his head down.

"Got it," Catherine says. She backs away from the door and smiles. Julia high-fives her.

Marco says, "You're amazing."

Catherine smiles really big, and Julia laughs and says, "Go get changed, kid."

Marco runs upstairs, and Julia and I mill around the kitchen and the living room. Catherine's hungry, so we let her go into the kitchen and root around Mr. and Mrs. Kimura's snack drawer. It's full of weird organic stuff.

Even though Marco's parents have been gone for less than a week, the house still feels cold and abandoned, like we're visiting a place in a ghost town. There are only tiny indications down here that the baby's coming home soon—rubber corners tacked onto the sides of the coffee table, big locks on the windows. I bet those are why we couldn't open them. But to be honest, I'm not sure

I would have noticed any differences in the house if Marco hadn't been forcing me to document every baby-related change to his life in my notebook ever since his parents first started calling his old playroom *the nursery*.

Julia plays with some of the trinkets Mrs. Kimura brought home from Italy. "Are you okay?" I ask. "With the thing?"

"The math camp thing?"

"Yeah."

Julia sits down on the couch. "Yeah. I'm getting there. My friends are right, you know? It *is* stupid to keep wishing for this thing that isn't going to happen. Remember in sixth grade, in health class, all the stuff they teach you about—"

For the love of God, please don't make me have a health class talk with Julia.

"—how you shouldn't try to be someone you're not?" She tucks a loose strand of hair behind her ear. "Well... isn't that what I'm doing, by trying out for math camp again and again? I'm trying to be this smart girl and that's just... it's not who I am."

"But it's who you want to be."

She laughs a little. "And you want to be Marco, but that doesn't mean it's going to happen."

I don't think either of us was prepared for how quiet and cold that would make the room seem, all of a sudden.

She shrugs and looks away, like she knows she caused it and she's embarrassed. "Maybe it's just time to stop hoping for things that don't make sense."

Except I can't agree with her, because all of tonight is about believing the golden boy soccer star is somehow in love with my angsty best friend.

I have to believe that. That's my job.

"I don't know," I say, quietly. Because part of me agrees with her. And I hate that.

She gets up and hugs me. "I'm sorry."

"I don't know why you're apologizing."

"Well, good," she says, and then she tweaks my nose.

My phone buzzes just then, and I fish it out of my pocket. It's Sherri. Her text says,

    marco won some award right?

    yes

    luke is on some forum for lacrosse
    players talking about how hes mad he

```
                didnt get it. not very good at keeping
                personal information personal. needs to
                get one of those lectures. idiot

                oh

                making threats

                what?

                Says the guy who got it didn't deserve
                it. weak or something. he means marco?
```

I type back thanks sherri. let me know if you find out anything more and save all the messages to my phone. I should forward them to Sasha, probably, but right now I just need to breathe.

Breathe.

Julia's watching me.

"What did he say to you?" I say. "You gave him money. What did he say to you?"

"He told me not to tell you."

"Julia."

"He said he told you he was going to get the money

from Luke, but then Luke told him how much he wanted the iPod and Marco just gave it to him. Says it's almost Luke's birthday and it seemed gentlemanly."

I flip through the notebook. It is almost Luke's birthday. Marco shouldn't know that from memory.

But Marco knows a lot of things about Luke. Knows them like he's forced himself to memorize them. Like maybe if he knows enough about Luke, Luke will be nice to him, or something. I don't know. I don't understand what's up with those two because I know how people act around people who push them around—I mean, let's be honest, Marco's not always great to me—and it's not what Marco does. Marco is hyperaware of Luke all the time. He always knows where he's sitting and stuff like when his birthday is, and he talks about him all the time.

Ugh, I hope Marco doesn't like him.

But then I look at Sherri's text again—*making threats*—and okay, how *Marco* feels about *Luke* really isn't the issue here.

Julia says, "What's going on?"

I say, "What should I do if I think someone's going to hurt Marco?"

"What? You should bring him home."

"He won't go. He'll fight. He'll run away."

"Not if he thinks he's going to get hurt. Stephen, what's going on?"

"You don't understand. *He* doesn't understand." I don't know what I'm saying. "He isn't thinking about this. All he cares about is getting to Benji. He's not worried about any of this, and that's fine, because Sasha is, and me. He doesn't see what's going on." I'm the one getting the text messages. I'm the one working on the case. I'm the one getting snow cones thrown at me. I'm the one who has this job.

And that's *fine*. Really. It's fine. It's totally fine. I can handle this.

Julia says, "You . . . then you have to protect him."

I nod.

Hard.

"Stephen?" Marco calls.

Deep breath. And out.

I have to protect him.

There's no point in telling him what's going on, in trying to scare him into listening to me. It wouldn't work, anyway. He wouldn't get scared. Marco doesn't get scared. He gets mad.

If I take him home, he'll climb out a window the second I turn my back. And he'll never, ever speak to me again.

"It's fine," I tell Julia. "It'll be fine."

"You need to tell someone, Stephen. Tell an adult."

"I will. I'll take care of it."

It's harder to lie to Julia than it was to Brian.

I can do this. I don't need help. I can do this all on my own. Marco's mission is to get the guy. Sasha's is to catch the criminal. All I have to do is help them out and keep Marco safe. I am going to be the hero of this one story that's happening tonight.

"Stephen?" Marco calls again.

I nod to Julia and follow his voice up the stairs. He's standing in his doorway, looking at himself in the mirror, exactly like he did in the tux shop. And he doesn't seem any more satisfied.

"You look good," I say.

"No I don't." He messes up his hair with the palm of his hand. He used to do that all the time when he was nervous, but I haven't seen him do it in a while. He stops pretty quickly and presses his palm into his forehead.

"You do," I say. "Don't stress."

"I don't look good. I look . . . fine."

I watch him in the mirror and try to act like I'm not thinking about it. But I think maybe he's right. He doesn't look bad, but he just looks like someone put him in a suit.

Sherri has these paper dolls that she dresses in different outfits by folding paper tabs around their bodies. I always think it's weird that they have the same expression when they're in the underwear as they do when they're in wedding dresses. Marco doesn't look dressed up as much as he just looks like someone shoved him into a suit. He's still Marco, and I don't think he wants to be right now. He wants to be James Bond.

The truth is, it's still kind of big on him.

And then he says, "I want to look like you." He sighs a little. "We can just leave our clothes here so we don't have to walk back to the school from the bus stop. So there's that at least. Saving time."

"Yeah." Ugh. That's not going to make meeting Sasha any easier. We'll still be going to school for the transfer, but we won't be sticking around.

He's scuffing his feet against the ground. "I really wanted to look good, you know?"

I stand behind him and dust some of the lint off his shoulders. "You know what you need?"

He shakes his head.

"Flower. Right here." I tug my lapel. "What're they called?"

"Boutonnieres. Girls are supposed to give them to you."

I try to shake the image of Sasha pinning one on me, and I say, "Well…that's not going to happen."

Marco laughs a little. "No kidding."

"So what do you say?"

He shakes his head. "It's not in the plan."

I take the notebook out of my pocket and add a note to the plan—*ADD FLOWER IF NECESSARY.* I show it to him.

"We have all this money leftover, now," I say. "From only getting one tux. So, we deserve it."

Marco looks at himself in the mirror, and I see him start to smile a little. I convinced him. I guess every once in a while, something impossible does happen.

But I guess he reads my mind, because he says, "This doesn't change that this whole thing is my idea. The whole plan. All of it."

"Whatever, Marco."

"I'm just saying. I'm the one making the plans."

"Yeah, I get it."

Seriously, no one knows how to ruin a moment like Marco does.

On our way out, Marco jumps to reach Julia's cheek and smacks a kiss there. "You're smarter than you think you are," he says to her. "You know way too much about people. It's impossible. You're impossible."

She rolls her eyes, but she's smiling.

"See ya, Catherine," I say.

"Are we getting on the same bus?" Julia says.

"No. We have a detour." I wave and start walking ahead, with Marco. I look over my shoulder just in time to see Julia mouth, *Take care of him.*

Yeah, I know. I also know he isn't going to make it easy.

And it starts to rain again.

ADD FLOWER IF NECESSARY (UNLESS YOU'RE MARCO, APPARENTLY)

"Are you sure this is the right bus?" Marco asks me. He's bouncing up and down a little. He rolled up the bottoms of his suit pants before we started sprinting from tree to tree on our way to the bus stop, and now they're hanging all soggy over his ankles.

I slump against the window. "For the love of God, Marco, yes. This takes us right to the supermarket. We catch the V bus at 8:10."

"We're going to be late. We won't get to the prom until like nine. Until like a million o'clock, practically. Eastern Standard Time."

"No one gets to the prom on time anyway."

But he's kind of right about a million o'clock, because *late* really is going to be an understatement, judging by the traffic. Marco's brilliant plan didn't take into account that traffic is totally stopped up thanks to the limos and the drunk teenage drivers. Our bus is crawling.

"The *band* gets there on time," Marco says.

"And they're not going to leave early, either. He'll be there."

Marco rubs his hands back and forth through his hair. "I'm all wet..."

"You look fine."

He mouths *fine* to himself and shakes his head in disgust, then stops and smiles a little. "Boutonniere."

"Yep."

"Flowers love water." He nods hard. "Yeah. Can I draw in the notebook?"

He's like Catherine on road trips. "Yeah, go ahead." It's not a toy, but whatever.

He takes the notebook and draws for a while. He's humming a The Floor Is Lava song to himself, so quietly that I don't think he realizes he's doing it.

"I wonder if they'll play new songs tonight," he says.

"Probably."

"Hopefully, Stephen, hopefully. Probably is bad luck, I think." He laughs just a little, but not in that mean way. "We don't need any more bad luck."

"Don't get the notebook all wet."

"I won't." He nods to himself. "Everything's going to be fine now," he says, softly.

We're almost there when my mom calls. I clear my throat and try to make it sound like I'm studying. And not on a bus. "Hello?"

"Stephen. Sweetie." My mom always does that. She calls, and then seems a little surprised that we're on the phone. I always feel like she just calls whichever one of us her finger speed-dials first and then waits to see which kid picks up.

"Hi. How's Robbie?"

"He's really not feeling well. Brian's taking him out on another drive. The roads in this rain, though . . ."

"Brian's a good driver."

"And he calms Robbie down better than anything. Sweetie, are you coming home soon? Do I need to pick you up from anywhere?"

"We have our bikes."

"I can fit them in the trunk. I don't like you out this late, especially on prom night. I'm sure it's crazy out there.

And it's been raining on and off all evening. I know you've been inside, so you don't know what a mess it is out there, I bet…"

I look out the window over Marco's head.

She says, "Are you going to be home soon?"

"Yeah. Pretty soon."

It's hardest to lie to Mom.

"And you're with Marco, right?" she says.

"Of course." I wouldn't lie about that. She knows that, right?

"Good. I don't want either of you alone. At least I know you're looked after this way."

Marco's writing something, now, instead of drawing, but he has the notebook tilted away from me so I can't see. He's chewing on his lip.

"Yeah," I say. "Looked after."

Marco's head snaps up. "I don't need looking after!"

"I'm going to call again in an hour if you're not home. Be home. Call me if I need to come get you. Let me come get you."

"We'll be home soon. Don't worry so much. Love you." I didn't mean to say it, but it's not as if Marco's never heard me say it before. He always looks a little shocked, though. I don't think they say it a lot in his family. It's not like they don't love each other. They do. They're just… quiet.

Mom says she loves me and I hang up. Marco closes the notebook after a while and hands it back to me, and the bus gets to our stop before I can find the page he was working on.

When we get into the flower section at Giant, the girl in the white apron tells us exactly what Nic did: it's prom night, and we are idiots for waiting this long. It's like no one in this town understands the value of a last-minute heist.

I say, "Just decapitate regular flowers and give them to us."

"We have tulips," she says. "Everything else is gone."

Marco groans.

"You'll make a statement," she says. "No one wears tulips. I'll go get 'em and you can have a look, okay?" She disappears into the back.

As soon as she's gone, Marco tugs on my arm and lowers his voice to almost a whisper, even though there isn't anyone around to hear us. "Tulips give me migraines." He's looking at me with his eyes all wide.

I say, "Seriously? How do you even *know* that?"

"Most flowers do..."

I can't believe this kid sometimes. I also kind of can't believe that I didn't know that, but that's really not the point right now.

I say, "So what are we even *doing* here?"

"You said it'd make me look nice…"

God. I mean…God. What do you even say to that?

Of course he only listens to me when I'm wrong. When he *knows* I'm wrong. Because then later when he gets to go, *See what happens when I listen to you?*

I say, "Okay. You should go wait by the door or something. I'll tell her we're not getting them."

"Let's try them on," he says. "At least see how they look."

"Are you kidding?"

"I'll be able to tell if I can take it. I will. Just *trust* me. Seriously, please."

"This is a bad idea."

"Stop."

"Marco—"

Marco raises his hands, and his face is really crazy, and I think maybe he's going to hit me, and I pull back, but he stops and runs them both through his hair. "Look," he says. His voice is so tight and still that I could pluck it like a string. "I'd really appreciate it if you'd just stop questioning everything I say, all right?"

"I haven't been—"

"Can you just try trusting me on one thing? Please? Or, I don't know, trust *anyone* but one of your siblings, maybe?"

I give up. It's so hard nowadays to figure out where he's coming from. I think maybe I've overdosed on Marco for now. He's been living at my house for a week, he's puking his drama all over my life, and he's jumping on me for everything I say.

Maybe my problem is *him*.

Maybe all the problems I have—that he's leaving, that he's always going to be the hero, that he was there when we found out the thing about my dad—maybe the thing that makes them all problems is *him*.

I look at him. He's scuffling at the floor with his nice shoes, looking quiet and angry.

Maybe we're too old for this.

The flower lady comes back with a load of purple tulips. She pins one on me and one on Marco, who sneezes pretty much immediately. I give him a look, but he pulls out some of the unused tuxedo money and goes, "We'll take them."

On the way out, before we plunge out from under the awning and into the rain, I look at my reflection in the store window and figure that this was a pretty great purchase, at least for me. My tux was starting to get a little droopy and damp. I hope I don't have to pay extra for that when I bring it back. At least the jacket's kept me somewhat dry, because even though it's June, it's gotten pretty cold now that it's dark.

Then the bus comes and we sprint across the street and up the steps, but the rain's coming down harder now and I'm pretty sure even a flower isn't going to do me much good. I'm going to look like I swam to the prom no matter what I do. I guess it doesn't really matter. Sasha will only see me in the dark, anyway.

I shake myself off a little before I sit down. Beside me, Marco's staring out the window and rubbing the bridge of his nose with his palm. He's shivering. I don't ask if he's okay. He'll tell me if he isn't. And if he doesn't tell me, it's not really any of my business.

And I probably care a little less than I should, yeah. But it's not like it's going to kill him, you know? It's a flower. I have his actual livelihood or whatever to worry about.

HALF-ITALIAN, HALF-SOGGY JERKWEASEL

Have info I text Sasha. On my way now.

She doesn't answer, but I knew I'd have to wait a minute. She texts even slower than my mom.

Next to me, Marco makes this noise in the back of his throat.

"Take the flower off," I say.

"Leave me alone." His eyes are closed, and he's pushing his forehead against the back of the seat in front of us. The rain made his skin all pale and clammy, and he pretty much looks like he's going to throw up any minute now.

"I don't have Tylenol."

He says, "I know."

"Okay, I get it. Flowers were a bad idea. I should shut up and let you have all the ideas. I get it. Take it off."

"That's not why I'm doing this!"

"Then what?"

"Shut *up!*" He looks up. "Okay. Fine. Just believe what you want. I don't care. Just *stop arguing with me. This isn't about you.*"

Someday I'm going to wake up and find out that Marco's tattooed that on the back of my hand, so I have to look at it all the time. *This isn't about you. This isn't about you. This isn't about you.*

I push my head back against the seat and breathe out. Really long, really slow. Breathe it all out.

He swallows. "Your voice hurts."

So I don't say anything.

No answer from Sasha.

Marco sneezes for the millionth time and presses one palm into his eye. He should stop trying to make his point and take the flower off. It's like he doesn't think I'll learn my lesson not to question his authority until he's dying in the gutter or something. I get it, okay? And I figured it out from *Julia*, not him.

I'm not trying to take control of this stupid heist.

I have my own thing going on. An actual problem. Keeping him safe is my actual problem.

But he doesn't think I have anything going on besides playing sidekick to him and Benji.

It's like he thinks I'm his puppy or something.

Maybe I am.

Maybe I let myself be. Maybe the real reason we've planned this whole mission to go after Benji and not Sasha is that Marco would never go along with a plan to woo Sasha.

Or maybe he knows I'm not the kind of guy who would ever go through with it. He thinks I couldn't handle it.

He thinks I can't be anything but a sidekick.

I have a lot to prove by telling her tonight, I guess.

My phone buzzes. Sasha.

> nice going, detective. when will you be
> here?

"Nice going, detective." I'm amazing.

The hard part is that we don't actually know what Luke's doing or what he's planning or where he's going to be, and the really hard part is that I don't have Marco as my assistant on this one. He's just this parcel I have to protect. I'm secret service right now instead of special agent, and this is a new role for me.

It isn't as fun as solving mysteries.

I check my watch. 8:13. We'll be at school by 8:20 at the latest. I'll send Marco in to wash his face and break into the nurse's office for some Tylenol and while he's inside I'll meet with Sasha. I'll get the stationery and we'll figure out the situation. Hopefully I'll be able to turn my detective skills on to their highest frequency and figure out how to catch Luke and get to the prom and get the note written up and keep Marco safe and not kill Marco and, somewhere in there, Sasha and I will make out.

5 minutes, maybe 10

No problem.

Then Marco starts coughing. It's stuffed-up and gross and sounds like it hurts. Geez. Over one flower. I look down at my lapel. Well, two flowers.

"I'm taking mine off," I say. I shake his shoulder until he looks at me, then I unpin the flower and stuff it into my backpack. "Look."

"Noooo," he says.

"Yeah, because it's bothering you."

"It's not bothering me." But he lets me wipe the gunk off under his nose with a tissue. "I'm fine," he says. "Just cold."

"You're a mess. Take yours off."

He pulls away. "I'm not a mess."

"Marco."

"Don't call me that."

"Call you Marco?"

"Mess," he says.

Whatever. I'm done with this. This is one situation where I know how to get what I want.

The truth is, Marco is really easy to play.

I close my eyes and rub my forehead, and he drops his voice way down. "You okay?" he says.

"You're driving me crazy. Giving me a headache." I don't have a headache really. I just know how to get to him.

He's quiet for a while, then in that same small voice, he goes "Sorry," and stares at the ground. He keeps one of his palms pushed into his temple. And sure enough, a minute later, he reaches up and takes his flower off and drops it in my backpack. He looks up at me and goes, "Did that help?"

I stop rubbing my forehead. "Yeah."

He smiles.

He really is so easy sometimes. I squeeze his shoulder.

A few minutes later, he's starting to look a little better, though I can tell his head's still bothering him. But he picks himself up enough to look out the window, and he says, "Stevey? Where are we?"

"What?"

"I don't recognize any of this."

I have to lean around him so I can press my forehead against the glass and see through our reflections. It's hard to figure out if anything is familiar, because all I can see are streets and shopping centers passing too quickly and a street lamp or two.

I say, "I think my sister used to have piano lessons around here."

He looks at me. "Around here?"

"Yeah."

"So . . . not around where we're going?"

My stomach feels like it's shrinking. "I guess not."

"Are we on the wrong bus?" Marco turns to me and goes, "*God,* Stevey! How could we get on the wrong bus?"

"I'm sorry. Seriously."

"I can't *believe* this! All you had to do was get us on *one bus*."

"I got us to the supermarket just fine!"

"God. *God*." Marco pushes me up into the aisle, then he grabs my arm and leads me to the front of the bus. "Excuse me?" he calls to the driver.

"Stay back," the driver says, like he's bored. He's talking on the phone, I think. That's so not allowed.

Marco says, "We need to find out—"

"Stay back," he says again, then he goes back to talking to someone on his phone in some language I don't know, but I can tell by the way Marco's face lights up that it's Italian.

"Ehi!" Marco yells, and then he's barking at the driver in Italian, so fast that even if he were only saying the ten words I know over and over again, I wouldn't be able to pick them out.

The driver puts down his phone and listens. I guess Marco can control a conversation in any language.

I've heard Marco speak Italian a million times, and I guess I should have grown out of thinking it's cool, but I totally haven't. And I still get a kick out of the looks on people's faces when they realize he can speak it, since people never have any clue what Marco is and never peg

171

him as Italian, even after he tells them his first name. They think it's all a hoax or something.

We should use that to our advantage in our next heist. Why do I have a feeling Marco wouldn't be into that?

Why do I even think there's going to be a next heist? Well, there's going to be exactly one more, and that's kind of the problem, I guess.

Our next heist is high school.

I look away from everything for a second.

Marco finishes talking with the driver and looks at me. He doesn't look mad as much as he just looks scrunched like a spring.

"Wrong bus?" I say.

He rubs his forehead. "We're supposed to be on V. This is U."

"Can we transfer?"

"Yeah. It's . . . actually going to be okay. We get off two stops from now and we can catch the V." He's trying and completely failing to calm down. "It's going to be fine."

The bus jerks a little, and I grab his arm so we don't fall over. "Let's sit down," he says. "I'm kinda dizzy."

"Good idea."

"I'm full of 'em," he says. He sounds tired.

been a delay I text Sasha. but we'll be there soon.

My phone buzzes pretty quickly afterward, but Marco snatches it before I can. "Oooh, who you teeeexting?"

"You're a girl. A five-year-old girl. Give me my phone."

"It's Sasha. She says *okay*. You know what that means."

"Shut up."

"She wants you. Madly and badly. She's deeply, madly, tragically in love with you. You're her favorite in the universe."

"You talk about favorites too much."

"Her favorite in the whoole universe." He's grinning at me, and I snatch my phone back, but I think I'm grinning, too. Because this is a moment that isn't so bad. And thank God it was this text message he saw and not one of the earlier ones.

Then the bus jerks again and it makes this hideous scraping sound and then stops.

No. No way.

Either Marco or the universe ruins everything in the whole world eventually. That's the lesson of tonight.

Marco looks at me with his eyebrows up under his bangs. "No way," he says.

"Oh my God."

Everyone on the bus looks at one another. It's always weird when you're in a public place and something goes wrong. I was at a museum with my family once, and the fire alarm started going off. First there's a minute when we all try to pretend we don't hear it, and then we all look at each other like we feel kind of guilty, and then all of a sudden we're grabbing everyone in line like we're old friends. When a minute ago, we were trying to pretend none of them existed.

The driver gets out of the bus without a word to us. We look out the window and watch him examine one of the wheels.

"Must be a flat," the guy behind us says.

"No," says the girl with him. "A flat wouldn't have made that kind of squeal."

"That wasn't a squeal."

"It was a squeal."

Marco stands up and says, "I'll find out what's wrong."

"I'm coming with you."

He shakes his head. "You stay here. Guard the camera and stay dry. I'm already freezing. We both don't need to go." He wraps his fingers around my wrist and squeezes, which is weird but actually kind of nice.

But still. "You don't know anything about cars," I say. "I can maybe figure it out."

He lets go. "It's not a car. It's a bus."

"Oh, okay, you're an expert then. Look, speaking Italian isn't going to help if you don't know the words for what the parts are. In *any* language."

"You don't know that! Maybe I can help!"

I stick the camera in my pocket and lug both our backpacks off the bus. He's crouching down, arguing with the bus driver in Italian.

I can't figure out where we are. The only light comes from two dim streetlamps and a bar and a pet store at the end of the street. Everything looks brown—the sidewalk, the buildings, the sky.

Marco looks up at me and says, "He thinks this tire might be flat."

I kick it, and the driver grumbles at me. "It's not flat," I say. "Hold on." I crouch down and look around the tire. If I could get under the bus, that would probably help, but there's no way I can fit unless we raise up the bus. And the driver doesn't seem capable of raising up a tricycle. "I think there's something wrong with the axle." I stand up and cross my arms and look at Marco. I'm waiting for him to ask me how I know that. To challenge whether I know what I'm talking about.

But he doesn't.

He's smarter than I give him credit for, I guess.

I'm remembering Stupid Sperm Whale telling me I was his favorite kid, that when it came to fixing old cars in the garage, I was worth two Brians. Three, even.

"So what do we do?" Marco says.

The bus driver gets back on the bus and starts waving everyone out.

"I don't know. I need to get up underneath to see what we're dealing with, even if he has the parts. And we couldn't get under there until they lift it up."

"Mechanic?"

"Yeah."

Marco curses and looks away from me.

Everyone's filing off the bus. "We'll have a new bus in forty-five minutes," he says. "They're sending one." Everyone starts grumbling.

Marco says, "We don't have forty-five minutes." He takes the camera and snaps a picture of the bus. It's probably going to come out awful because he's shaking.

I say, "We don't have any other choice."

Then Marco does something weird. He acts like he's about to say something, maybe even about to agree with me, and then he looks around us really hard. Like he's trying to memorize everything. He stands up as tall as he can and looks around at everything.

Then he says, quietly, "We're not that far from where we were going to transfer, right? Like a stop and a half. We walk there, we get on a bus, and we're right at school. Drop our stuff off, go. We'll be at the prom before that other bus could even get here."

"You know which way to go?"

"Yeah. I do."

"How?"

He shrugs, which is not an answer.

I take a deep breath and let it out. "Okay. If you say so."

So while everyone else mills around the broken-down bus, Marco leads me up the hill toward a pet store.

We've walked for about five minutes, completely silently, when I see everything's getting darker and darker and the streets are getting narrower and narrower. "I'm scared," I say. The words are out before I can stop them.

He looks at me. "Stephen, come on." His voice is twisted in disgust.

"Can we go back?"

"Go *back*?"

"To the bus. Where there are ... people."

He stops. "Look, Stevey. I get it. This is creepy. But you need to pull yourself together, okay? I know where we're going. This is ... this is the real deal. This."

"What are you talking about?"

He breathes out, like I'm the one bothering him. It's starting to rain again. Awesome.

"This is growing up," he says. "Going on our own. Not waiting for the bus."

I don't want to talk about this.

"No, you are supposed to be the one who wants to talk about this," Marco says.

Which is incredible, because I didn't say that last thing out loud.

I think he's been wanting to have this argument with me for a long time.

"You're the one who was enthusiastic about this," he says. "And I wasn't scared because you weren't scared. You said, 'It's just high school; it's not going to change anything.' And then the second I thought it would be okay, you changed your—"

"You decided it was okay when you decided you were *leaving*!"

He stares at me and swallows. "You're so stupid, you know that?"

"Okay, fine! I'm stupid! Explain it to me, Marco! Explain to me why you're so happy to be going to your fancy new rich-boy school."

"Do we have to do this now?"

"How about explaining to me why you're going at all?"

"I don't know, Stephen. Maybe I'm doing it just to ruin your life!" He throws his arms out. His voice is loud because of the rain. "You've figured it out. You caught me. I'm leaving *just to teach you a lesson.*"

I cross my arms. Tighter.

"You might as well be," I call back.

"If I were going to teach you a lesson, you know what it would be? It would be yeah, that this is real life, that we're walking away from the bus and that's real life. This is it. Big real big scary life, without Brian or Julia there to hold your hand."

Julia will be in high school with me, but I guess that isn't the point. Or maybe it is the point, but Marco would yell at me if I brought it up.

Maybe *that's* the point.

He says, "This is real life, and real life doesn't have brothers and sisters holding your hand. You know what it has? It has me."

"How do you even know where we're going?"

"Keep walking."

On the next block, I nearly collide with one of those fancy brick signs on the sidewalk.

Clinton Preparatory Academy.

No wonder he knows this neighborhood.

He puts his hands in his pockets and doesn't look at me. And that sign is just staring me in the face, and I really, really can't pretend it isn't here.

So, yeah. I guess we have to do this now.

BEST FRIENDS ARE FOR PEOPLE WHO LIKE GETTING CLOBBERED

It's not that seeing the school told me something I didn't know. It's not like it's revealed some secret motive for why we're here or why Marco's leaving or why he's in love with Benji or why anyone does anything.

It's just that I really didn't need one more bad thing to think about right now, and it's literally right here in front of me.

But it's Marco who starts it. Who says in this really quiet voice, "Why isn't this fun anymore?"

"What?"

"Heists."

Because we're sick of each other. I don't know.

"Because it's our last one," I say.

He stares at me for a minute. Then he says, "Seriously? That's it? *All* of this is about me changing schools?"

"All of what?"

"This." He gestures toward me. "The attitude. The arguing. This whole . . . thing you've been doing all night."

I will not strangle him. I will not strangle him. I'm supposed to be keeping him safe.

"Stevey," Marco says. "Do you think I want to do this? Do you honestly think I want to leave you and Benji and Sasha and Julia and *everybody*?"

He sits down on the curb and holds his head, which would be a lot more dramatic if his suit weren't already a mess and if I didn't know he was doing it just because he has a headache.

He says, "Do we have to think about this tonight? No. We don't. So we're not going to think about this tonight. We're going to have one night of things exactly how they're supposed to be, with none of the awful in the whole awful world having anything to do with us." He stands up. "Come on. We're not going to think about this."

"I'm thinking about this."

"Stop."

"I can't, okay? I guess I'm petty and stupid and I'm

your clingy little best friend. But this is stupid. Running around lost in the rain—"

"We're not lost."

"—in this tux that's going to cost me a fortune now to return, and you have a headache, and we're doing this for some guy, and you're telling me this is supposed to be some kind of going-away party for us? This is stupid. This is all stupid."

Marco is perfectly still for a minute. Then he stands up and backs away from me a few steps. "Fine," he says.

It's so dark behind him. My heart is all of a sudden beating so hard it hurts. I don't know what's behind him. I can't let him go. I have to keep him safe.

"What are you doing?" I say.

"I'm leaving. I'm doing this on my own. Call your mom to pick you up."

"You can't do that."

"This is just about me and Benji, right? This has nothing to do with us? Then it doesn't matter. I can do it better on my own anyway, I bet. Why did you even come?"

Because you said you wanted me to.

"I can't let you go on your own," I say.

"What?"

"You're not going anywhere without me."

"You just said you—"

"Why didn't you get the money from Luke?"

He shakes his head a little. "What?"

"Why do you let him push you around?"

"I don't—"

"You're not freaking safe, okay?"

He stops taking steps backward. He stares at me. He doesn't say anything.

I say, "Luke bashed in your locker, and Sasha and Sherri and I looked into it and ... and he's not happy just bashing in your locker and leaving notes on Mr. Takeda's desk. He wanted that award, and he's mad at you for getting it, and I guess he's mad at Mr. Takeda for choosing you, and you know he knows you're out tonight and that the town's a mess with the prom and that you don't have anyone but me looking out for you, okay? If something were going to happen ... you're getting the award *tomorrow*, you're vulnerable *tonight*, come on."

"You're overreacting."

"No."

Marco shakes his head. "Luke wouldn't ... no. Luke wouldn't do that. Wouldn't actually hurt me. Real world hurt me." He shakes his head. "He couldn't. That couldn't happen to me."

"Why are you sticking up for him? Do you like, do you have a crush on him or something?"

Marco stares at me.

I probably shouldn't have said that, because I can tell from his expression that I could not be more wrong if I tried.

He says, "You think I have a crush on Luke? Stephen. Are you kidding me right now?" His voice actually breaks a little. But he can do it on purpose. So I don't know.

"I don't know," I say.

Marco looks like he's going to say something, but then he just shakes his head and says, very quietly, "He can't hurt me for real," Marco says. He's really quiet. "It can't, it can't happen, it...I decided a long time ago that wouldn't happen to me."

That doesn't make sense.

"That's why I'm keeping you safe," I say. "That's why I'm here. So if you could stop freaking drama-queening out about—"

His head snaps up. *"Drama-queening?"*

"—this little prom thing, okay? It's not important anymore. You want to talk real life? *This* is real life, okay? Having to keep you safe is real life. And I'm trying to let you have your little night, but *God* you are so frustrating, and I don't care about the prom, okay? I don't care. I don't care if Benji finds out you like him. I don't care whether or not Benji likes you. None of that is important. What's important is that you are safe. Right now. I'm here to be your bodyguard, so you do whatever, and you yell and you try to walk away and I'll just be here. And you are driving me insane and honestly I don't know why I care that you're safe. Right now, I really don't know why I care. Except you're going to be. Safe. And you are not going anywhere without me. No matter how much either of us wants you to. Okay?"

Marco still hasn't moved.

I say, "You're scared. I know. I'm sorry. I . . . didn't want to scare you with this. Sasha told me not to."

"You came to *be my bodyguard*?"

I can't believe this.

He's not scared.

He's mad.

He says, "You're my bodyguard because *Sasha told you to be*?"

"This is the stupidest thing in the world to be mad at me about. You realize that, right? You should be thanking me."

"I don't need you. What, because I'm *small*? So I need

someone to hold my hand and keep me safe from the bad guys? You get *that* but you don't get why I have to change schools?"

"What?"

"Gee, thanks, Stephen. Thank you *so much*." He shakes his head. "I'm going. I'm going to be late as it is." He shakes his head more. "I guess you're coming with me."

"I guess so."

"Fine. Then let's go."

I hate that I almost don't follow him.

GETTING CLOBBERED

"Did Luke ever hurt you?" I say, after a minute.

He doesn't look at me or stop walking.

So I say, "One time he kicked me. Right behind the knees while I was walking. In sixth grade, right when everyone found out you were gay."

"Yeah." He doesn't say it with any expression.

"I fell and scraped my hands up pretty bad. But that's it. You don't have to be afraid of him, you know? He's this stupid kid who kicks people behind the knees."

What I'm really saying is *I'll be afraid for you,* I guess.

Marco shakes his head.

"Did he ever hurt you?" I say.

"No."

"You don't have to be afraid."

"Why are we still talking?" He shivers and shoves his hands under his armpits.

I say, "If you really think Luke wouldn't actually hurt you..."

"I didn't say that."

"You did, though."

He doesn't say anything. "I don't know. It's not like we've ever had an in-depth discussion about it. So I'm glad you and I are hashing this out. Make sure to write this all down in the notebook and we'll turn in the minutes to Luke later. Or to Sasha, right?"

I don't say anything.

He stops and looks at me. "Be the bodyguard. I don't care. But make me a deal. We don't talk about this anymore. We don't let this ruin my night anymore. We make this about Benji again. Okay?"

"Fine. Whatever." I don't care.

"I can't see anything."

"The fence is here." I put his hand on it.

He says, "Oh." Then his foot goes down in a puddle, deep, and that's like the final straw in pretending we're going to look anything close to presentable.

He shivers again, gives his forehead a hard rub, and goes, "Stevey, I—"

Someone whistles, long and high, somewhere to our left. We both jump a little.

"What was that?" he says.

I hear a car door slam shut and a few people start to walk toward us. They're talking quietly and laughing.

Marco curses in Italian.

I say, "What's going on?"

"Follow my lead, okay?" he says. "Stay behind me."

He's like four feet tall, though.

It's three people, and they walk toward us without stopping. One is that kid Chris who threw one of the slushies at us. One is a girl who used to go to our school—I don't remember her name and I haven't seen her in a long time—and the other looks older and I don't know who he is, but he's tall and he's walking straight at me.

They back us right into the fence and grab our arms. The whole thing takes about five seconds from when we first spotted them.

"Well, look who's here," Chris says.

Marco says, "Luke said you'd leave us alone tonight."

"Looks like Luke lied, huh?" His face is right up against Marco's.

Marco doesn't say anything. I don't hear anything in the whole world but his breathing.

I'm looking at the guy holding me back. His hood is so far over his face that I can't see his eyes. He doesn't look like a real person. And I'm not trying to make out his face or take notes in my head for the case file. It doesn't even matter if I knew what he looked like because I would have nothing if I did, because this is so completely far from a game.

Marco breathes in and out.

"Nice suit," the girl says, running her finger underneath Marco's jacket.

"Stop," he says.

The older guy shakes his head at her and turns back to me. "Money."

Chris says, "Yeah, sure, might as well. Marco. Money."

I turn my head as much as I can to look at Marco. He's shivering and staring at Chris. But he doesn't look scared, just mad.

"Money," the tall one says again. He flicks my chin and makes me look at him.

The tall boy jabs me in the stomach with his other hand. "Money."

"You don't have *any* money?" His fist is pushing harder into my stomach.

I shake my head. My hair makes a scraping noise against the brick. It sounds like a scream. "We get on the bus free with student ID—"

He jabs my stomach, hard, and I lose my voice and my breath.

Then Marco does the stupidest thing he's ever done.

He wrenches his arm away from Chris and he grabs my hand.

Chris snatches Marco's hand from mine and waves it at the girl. "See, Caitlin? I told you." He pushes at Marco's pulse point to make his wrist go limp. Marco immediately bends it back the way it was.

Caitlin says, "Aw, are you guys on the way to your wedding?"

The big guy laughs and twists his fist in my gut, then he reaches inside my jacket and starts patting down my sides. I don't know what he's doing.

"Get off of him," Marco says. "Get off."

Then the guy punches me, hard, right at the base of my ribcage.

I hear my body make a noise like a drum, then Marco yelling, "I have money! He doesn't have any; I have all of it."

The big guy takes one of his hands off me. "Yeah?"

"Eighty dollars in the wallet in my front pocket." Marco's watching me while he talks.

They argue about who has to be the one to reach into Marco's pocket. Then Chris finally dives in and comes up with his wallet. He counts the money out and searches Marco's pockets for anything else interesting. He rejects his phone. It's cheap and old.

"Anything good on him?" he asks the big guy, with a nod at me.

"Phone. Camera."

Chris is about to say something, but he shuts his mouth as his phone starts to ring. He takes a few steps away from us and talks quietly. The girl takes his place in front of Marco, but she very obviously doesn't want to touch him.

I can't stop coughing. Marco doesn't try to touch me, thank God.

Chris turns back around and says, "It's time," and then they're gone. Each of them gives Marco's cheek a little smack on their way by. He doesn't flinch.

My stomach hurts like the big guy's fist is still there. They didn't take my stuff.

Marco rubs his palms down his face. Then he crouches down next to me. He says, "Oh my God. Are you okay?"

I am, but I don't have enough breath to say it yet, and Marco doesn't seem to notice anyway. He's not even looking at me anymore. "God!" he says. "God! They took my wallet! My dad brought me that wallet from Milan!"

Because that's what he cares about. Of course. I get a second of concern and then it's his wallet.

The only surprise is that I'm surprised.

As soon as I can talk, I go, "Why did you grab my hand?"

He looks at me. "I—"

"They hit me because you grabbed my hand!"

It's not fair. I can't stand this anymore. Why am *I* always the one who gets beat up about Marco? He gets his locker destroyed, fine, but I'm the one getting stuff thrown at me and getting punched in the stomach and what do I get out of it? I get a friend who treats me like his lapdog and sulks in the back of my Hebrew school class and doesn't really care about me at all. I get pushed around by people trying to get to him, and then I turn around and get pushed around by him, and it keeps going and going and I don't have *anyone*.

I've been taking hits for him and taking hits from him every single day of my life since I was five years old, and he won't even listen to me when I suggest we should go back, and yeah, Marco, maybe I know a thing or two about Luke because I know a thing or two about bullies, and that did *not* all come from watching things people do to him. It didn't. Some of it came from him.

That's just a fact, and I'm tired.

We should have gone back.

They could have killed him.

"Stevey," Marco says, really quietly.

I look up at him.

"Are you okay?" he says.

I swallow. "Did they hurt you?"

He shakes his head.

"Okay. Then we're okay."

I want to get up to the school where there's some light, and then I'm going to call Brian. I'm going to tell him to get over here and pick us up.

Marco scoots a little closer to me. We can both pretend he's doing it because it's cold. It's okay.

Marco'll understand. The prom thing was a cute idea, but it's way more important that he's safe right now than that he's happy. He knows that. He's not dumb.

We'll go home and pretend this never happened. I'll

get Brian to bring the tux back. I'll tell Mom she didn't hear us come in way before curfew. I'll pretend I wasn't the world's worst bodyguard.

We'll pretend none of this ever happened.

"Let's get out of here," I say, and Marco nods. He follows behind me and doesn't say anything.

HE GOT AWAY

We want to take a different way from Chris and his friends, so we take the long way around the hill up to the school. We don't talk. We jump at our reflections and look over our shoulders at every rustle. At least it's not raining anymore. The prom started an hour ago, but Marco hasn't mentioned it. He's being much quieter than I am.

We hike up the hill. I don't see anyone here, not even Sasha. I hope she didn't go home. Or that Chris and the guys didn't get her. God.

But she's tough. She knows karate.

Marco wipes his nose on the cuff of his jacket. I wonder if he even realizes he's doing it. "Give me your stuff," he says.

"What?"

"I'll run it in. I need to stick my head under the hand dryer anyway. My hair must look horrible. How's your stomach?"

It takes me a minute to realize he means where I was punched. "It's fine," I say.

He looks down and nods.

"I can't figure out if we're fighting right now," he says, quietly.

I breathe out. "Me neither. Go inside and get everything, okay?"

He looks kind of confused. I look away from him and scan the front steps. I don't see Sasha.

He stiffens. "What are you looking for?"

I don't answer, and he sighs and goes around to the loose door behind the gym. He's only gone for a few seconds when I hear a soft voice say my name, and there she is, right by my ear.

Julia was pretending to be in disguise, but Sasha really is. Her sunglasses are even bigger and darker, and the brim of her hat is pulled down over her forehead. If the hair pulled back in her bun weren't Cherry Coke red, I might not recognize her.

She slips an envelope into my hand. "And what do you have?"

I shake my head. "I have to get him home. Chris and everyone grabbed us on the way in. Punched me in the gut."

Sasha puts her hand on my arm.

Whoa.

"Are you all right?" she says.

"Yeah, I'm fine. Of course."

"Was Luke there?"

"No. But he's behind this. He's got to be." I scroll through my phone and show her Sherri's text messages. Once she's done, I scroll through my contacts to find Brian's number. I should have it memorized, but I don't.

Sasha says, "Someone was here earlier. Twenty minutes ago, maybe. Dark clothes, couldn't see who it was. Not Luke. Looked like he was scoping the place out. I hid."

"Probably the guy who hit me."

"Or another one of them, yeah." She crosses her arms. "And look. I took this when I was getting the stationery." She shows me a picture of the secretary's office. There's the stationery, and next to it the attendance book where we have to sign in if we're late. There's Luke's name. "That's the handwriting," she says. "The shaky writing from the note on Mr. Takeda's desk. Right?"

I nod. "That's totally Luke's handwriting." And the same handwriting on the note I found on the ground by Marco's locker. Case closed.

"I guess we should tell someone."

I say, "We'll take care of it tomorrow."

"What about tonight?"

I look at her. "I told you. I have to get him home."

"But they were lurking around here. I don't think this is over. We're just going to leave and let them break in? We should call the police."

"Luke hasn't done anything yet. We don't have any evidence of anything but some writing on a locker."

"He hit you."

"Luke didn't hit me. And one punch? No one's going to get in trouble for that."

She says, "So stick around here with me. We'll catch them all in the act. We'll take pictures." She lowers her shoulders. "Unless you're going to the prom."

"We're not going to the prom. The prom is not in the equation right now. Marco knows that. He's scared to death."

She says, "So I guess you want to go home then."

"I...guess we could hang out here for a little while first." I have no idea how I'm going to talk Marco into this.

But being here with Sasha makes me feel like I could do anything.

She smiles, then says, "You did well. With the investigating."

"Thanks." It was totally Sherri, but I don't think she'd mind my taking credit. It's not like she has a crush on Sasha.

"You're really the best detective ever," Sasha says.

My brain just broke open, and all these singing birds rose out of the chasm. My whole world is this little curl poking out of Sasha's bun.

She thinks I'm the best detective ever.

She likes me.

Then I hear Marco's shoes squishing through the mud, then he goes, "Hey. Hey, Sasha, what are you doing here? You look cool."

She looks at me. "We were just..."

"Um..."

Marco crosses his arms.

I say, "Hey, do you mind if we stick around here for a minute before we go home?"

"When? After prom?"

Okay, so maybe I'm an idiot, but I really didn't think he was still planning on prom. Even though he was complaining about his hair. I thought that was just Marco keeping his game face on. Game hair.

He takes a piece of paper off the top of the stack I'm holding. "Is this the stationery?"

"Yeah."

"You didn't have it yet? I thought she gave it to you this morning."

"Relax, okay? I have it now. It doesn't matter now."

Marco says, "What's that other stuff?" and before I can stop him, he grabs the photos out of my hand. And then my phone. And he's looking at the picture and scrolling through the text messages. He's making this face like he's confused, but I know he gets what's going on. He's a good detective. But he keeps staring like the texts are in some language he doesn't understand.

"Why are you doing this?" he says.

Sasha points to the picture of Luke's handwriting. "See, this matches the handwriting on—"

He crumples the picture in his hand. "I don't care."

"What are you *doing*?" I say. "That's our evidence!"

"It's stupid. It's a stupid case, and it's not what we're doing here. That's *not our mission.* It's a who-cares picture of a who-cares attendance book. I told you I didn't want to talk about this tonight. Are we going?"

"He bashed in your locker," Sasha says.

"Yeah, Sasha, I know. Thanks." He looks at me. "Are we going?"

I look at Sasha, "I'm sorry," I say.

"No, it's okay," she nods. "I can handle it here."

"Okay," I give Marco's arm a shake. "Let's go home."

He pulls my arm away from me. "What is up with you? We're going to prom."

"You're kidding me right now. After what just happened to us... after what just happened to *me*, Marco, you still want to go back out there with, like, idiots wandering around, waiting for Luke's friends to beat us up again? To beat *me* up again?"

"We're going to prom!" He starts toward the bus stop. Sasha starts to say something, but I'm already following Marco. I think because I'm too shocked to do anything else. But after a few steps toward the bust stop, I find my voice.

"What are you *thinking?*" I yell at him. "This isn't a heist, okay? This is a suicide mission."

"So we should just stand around the school and let him get us here?"

"No, we should go home, but..." But... "This is our chance to fix this. This is our shot. To get back at him."

He doesn't turn around to look at me. "Let it go, Stephen."

I can't believe this. "Yeah, I'll just do that, Marco. I'll just forget all about it." I'm being sarcastic, but I still hear these words and realize I must have said them a million times before. Except then, I meant them. I would give up everything I cared about just so I wouldn't have to argue with him.

But not tonight.

Marco says, "It's my locker, and my business, and I told you to drop it."

"It's *my mission! I'm* going to fix it! Let me just do this one thing."

He stops walking so suddenly that I walk straight into him. We both spring backward like we electrocuted each other.

His face is all screwed up. "You think these hate crimes are about *you?*"

"Come on, I didn't say that. I think solving them was about me, okay? I think I finally did something without you, so you're trying to ruin it. Now can we please just forget it and go home?"

He laughs in the back of his throat. He's not looking at me. "God. Grow up, Stephen."

"You couldn't even let me have this one thing!"

Then he snaps his eyes up to my face. "*That's not what tonight is about!* Tonight is about you and me getting to prom. It's not about the hate crimes. This is about *us. Not them.*"

I've put up with a lot of Marco's lies over the years, but there is no way I'm going to take this one. I'm screaming. "Give it up, *God!* Stop *saying that!* Don't even ... this is about you and *Benji!* This has nothing to do with me." Now my chest hurts, and I'm losing my voice from screaming but I can't stop. I can't. "This has nothing to do with me, and it never does, and the one time I do something on my own—*I solved the mystery, I got you through being mugged without a freaking scratch*—you have to go and ruin it. I put up with so much. I go through *so much* for you, and you won't even let me catch the guy who's been torturing you. He's been *torturing* you, Marco. And I'm going to actually do something, to make something better, and this is so much more important than trying to confront some guy who probably doesn't even like you—"

"*Shut up!*"

"Luke is the one you should be mad at, okay? You're yelling at me while I always, always, tolerate—"

"*Tolerate?*"

I think something inside Marco just stretched so hard it broke. He has never looked this big before.

"*Tolerate?*" he screams again. "I'm not here to be *tolerated*!"

"Yeah, well, I have to, okay?" I'm right in his face, pushing him in the chest. I hear Sasha running up behind me and calling my name, but I can't focus on anything except how much I hate my best friend. "I put up with your whining about every single part of every single day and put up with your treating me like garbage whenever I'm inconvenient and, yeah, I put up with getting my fingers slammed in lockers and getting snow cones thrown in my face and getting called your boyfriend and getting ignored by girls and you won't even sit through Hebrew school for—"

"Poor baby!" Marco takes a few huge steps back and throws out his arms. "Poor, poor baby." He laughs again, that sick one in the back of his throat.

And he talks so slowly.

He says, "You go through so, so much, don't you? God, it's almost enough to make me forget that *I'm* the one who doesn't get to brush it off when the guys are mean to me. I'm the one who has to live with them every day. I don't get to go home after school and forget about it, and I can't open up a newspaper or a freaking web page without reading about someone else who wishes I would die or get the gay electrocuted out of me, and I'm the one who has to be grateful for anyone who *tolerates* me, to think that they're so perfect and open-minded because they're sweet enough to be *okay, I guess* with me. And I'm the one who has to deal with the ones who aren't okay with me, the ones not in the newspaper or on the Internet but *right here in my face all the time* who won't give me a second without telling me they're not okay with it, who leave letters in my backpack that say FAGS ARE GONNA DIE and I'm the one switching schools because of this crap, okay?"

He wipes his eyes, hard. I didn't even know he was crying.

I wish it were raining, just so it wouldn't be so quiet.

So I wouldn't have to think of something to say.

"Marco," Sasha says, really quietly. I'd forgotten she was there.

"Leave me alone," Marco says. "Go play with your girlfriend. I'm done."

And he's gone.

He's gone because I can't figure out what words to say, because there is no way to say *I'm sorry* and *I'm still mad* and *but I'm different* and *I will kill Luke for that note* all at the same time.

THIS IS HOW THINGS HAPPEN IN REAL LIFE

We look around the bottom of the hill for a while to see
if we can find Marco, but it's pretty clear he's long gone.
He's fast when he wants to be. It's the athlete part of
him. It's how he got that award.

He isn't answering his phone. And neither is Brian,
because I guess that's just how my life works.

Sasha and I shake ourselves off and pretend the "girlfriend" thing never happened, and we decide there's nothing better to do right now than catch the criminals. We
sneak back into the school and slip into the supply closet
in the gym. The whole time, she's looking over her shoulder at me. She has this really funny look on her face, like
I'm not who she was expecting to see.

I can't even pay attention, because I have way too many feelings (Marco left, Marco's a jerk, Marco better be okay), but the truth is that I'm the one in the line of fire here if something really is about to happen, so let's focus on me for a minute, okay? And I'm sick of feeling guilty about that. I'm done.

Yeah, right.

He'll be fine. He's always fine.

Sasha closes the door of the storage closet almost all the way, leaving a few inches open so we can see the back door of the gym. If anyone comes in through that back door, we'll see them.

If no one comes, this is going to be really embarrassing.

She looks at me and says, "It should be soon. Now that it's really dark out."

Dark. Marco. Alone.

I am a terrible bodyguard.

I hope he's okay.

She says, "Stephen? Are you okay?"

"I'm fine." I say it too fast. I already knew she wouldn't believe me, but I thought maybe I would.

"I know you hate fighting with him," she says. "Do you want to talk—"

"I like you."

210

Oh my God. What?

What did I just do?

She's staring at me. In my head, I'm screaming at her to say something, but I guess she can't hear it.

Oh my God, say something. Anything.

She doesn't. So I clear my throat and say, "So that's why Marco called you my girlfriend, I guess. I mean. Not that you're my girlfriend. But... I like you."

She looks down. "Oh."

I'm getting a really horrible hot bubbly feeling in my stomach. Not a good one. Not a good one at all.

Oh.

This is bad.

She rubs the back of her head with the palm of her hand. She's ruining her bun. She doesn't look like a character in a movie anymore.

She says, "Stephen... you're a really nice guy..."

Ohhhhh God.

"But I just never thought of us as anything more than friends... and I think maybe... see, you're *such* a good friend, and I'd hate to ruin that..." She keeps on going, but she's just saying the same thing over and over. No. No. No.

What was I thinking?

The pretty girl will never fall in love with the sidekick. The soccer star will never fall in love with the tiny kid pining on the sidelines. My sister will never be a genius. Brian will never be happy. I will never be the one to save the day.

There is no reason to expect that anything will change.

That I will change.

"I'm sorry," Sasha says. But she doesn't look sorry. She looks like she's afraid I'm going to grab her and kiss her.

"It's okay," I say, as fast as I can. "It's totally okay. I mean, I just meant like, I like you as a friend. So."

She nods. "Of course, yeah."

"So we can just forget this happened."

She keeps nodding. "Yeah, totally."

I don't know if we can.

Before I have time to think about it anymore, I hear the crack of the gym door, and Sasha puts her finger over her lips. We lean toward the door and listen while footsteps scurry through the gym and right past us. I can't figure out how many people there are, but it's definitely at least two. Luke isn't alone.

I see the treads of his sneakers running past us, and despite everything, I feel excitement in my throat when I see them. We did figure it out. We really did. I was right. The shocking twist isn't who it is.

The shocking twist is this moment right now when we look at each other and realize we have no idea what happens next.

Usually I bail as soon as the mystery's over. We tell the authorities, we shake hands, we get out. It's not like I've talked to my dad since the whole thing. We don't do after-math. We don't do the sentencing.

"Ready?" Sasha whispers to me.

No. But I nod.

We slowly open the door and trail their footsteps down the hall. We're so, so quiet.

My hands are glued to my camera.

We follow them to the auditorium and lurk outside the doors while they run around inside. There are crashes while they knock over a few tables, then the hiss of a can of spray paint.

"Now," Sasha whispers.

We throw open the auditorium doors, and I start rapid-fire photographing, my finger pumping up and down on the shutter button as fast as I can. If this were an action movie, and my camera were a machine gun, I would be the hero right now.

To be honest, I feel like the hero anyway.

I get a million pictures of Luke and Chris and that

kid Jason from my math class with sharpies and bottles of spray paint and their hands all over Marco's portrait and the word *HOMO* sprayed across my best friend's forehead.

Then they start charging toward us.

"Are you *insane?*" Luke's screaming. He turns to Chris. "You said you took care of them!"

"I'm about to take care of them," Chris says, in a voice he's probably practiced a million times and God does it do its job. I feel scared down to my bones.

"You're dead," Luke says. He gives me a small smile. "You're dead. Now what?"

I realize that Luke isn't much bigger than Marco.

He couldn't hurt anyone.

He makes his friends do it.

He's a coward.

Interesting.

But before I can figure out how to use that to my advantage, Chris steps toward us, cracking his knuckles. Jason starts laughing like a wild animal.

"We're dead," I tell Sasha.

"Run!"

Then we're tearing down the hallways, past our lockers, past Mr. Takeda's classroom. Their footsteps are behind us, and somehow they're building speed while we're panting and slowing down. We run down the halls and loop around, and before I know it we're back outside the auditorium again. They're right behind us, and I feel like I can't breathe.

Sasha stops, hard, and braces herself in front of the auditorium doors. "Stand back," she says.

"What?"

She holds me back with one arm and waits for the guys to get close to us. They skid to a stop. They hesitate. I guess they didn't really know what they were going to do when they caught us. Especially if they had to go through Sasha first. Are they really going to hit a girl?

So they hesitate, and the second they do, Sasha whips her leg around and kicks Chris square in the chest.

Right.

Chris rears back, and Jason starts toward me, but Sasha stops him with a punch in the stomach before she turns back to Chris and kicks him behind the knees.

Luke stares at me. His eyes are darting around, like he's thinking of running away.

I need to do this one myself.

And if I could do it without any violence, the way he does, I would. If I could figure out exactly how to stand

and what quiet, terrifying thing to lean in and say into his ear, if I had any idea how he manages to scare my best friend to death without laying a finger on him, I would do it that way.

But I don't.

And I'm glad that isn't a thing I know how to do. Because hitting Marco would have hurt him a lot less, all in all. And I'm not out to do some lasting psychological harm to Luke. I just want him to stop. Now.

So when he finally makes up his mind to come toward me for real, I throw myself at him and push him out into the hallway. I pin him against a row of lockers. My arms are across his chest like one of those overhead seat belts on a roller coaster. He's not going anywhere.

He's fighting, but I am so strong right now that I could keep him here forever.

"This ends now," I whisper at him.

I hear Chris groan as Sasha kicks him again. I'll let her handle him.

I let Luke go a little just so I can slam him back into the lockers. I want to drive my fist into his stomach, but I also know why I want to do that, so I don't. That's pay back for a crime that wasn't quite his, and he's done enough that I can stick to dishing out only exactly what he deserves.

"Marco got that award because they felt sorry for him," he says. "Mr. Takeda played favorites with the queer little—"

"Shut up. You shut. Up. You bashed in his locker. You put notes in his backpack. You took his iPod. You teased him. You humiliated him. *He is changing schools because of you and your horrible friends.*"

And I should have known that from the start.

Luke says, "That should have been my award! I was going to win something! I was going to get that plaque and I was going to go into high school with people knowing me, and it was going to be perfect, and then he went and—"

"You want to be seen? You want to be noticed?" I say.

I grab the sharpie out of his pocket. And I hold him still with my arm and my knee while I write *JERKWEASEL* on his forehead.

"What are you doing?" Luke's screaming, and he's cursing at me and pushing against me, but I'm not moving.

Because I'm busy being a good best friend.

Because every once in a while, the sidekick gets to be the hero, it turns out.

"Get *off* me!" Luke yells. He grabs my arm and pries it

off of him. Then he takes a swing at my face, but I get away in time. I twist his arm, all the way behind his back, and he screams while I hold his wrists in place and kick him front-first back into the lockers. He groans when his chest hits so hard the padlocks rattle.

That felt good.

I look at Sasha by the doors to the auditorium. Both the guys are on the floor, and she's standing over them like a warrior. Whoa. She cranes to look at Luke's forehead, then nods. "Nice tag."

"Thanks."

She pants and looks at the guys on the floor. "Now what?"

That's a good question. I have no idea. Once we let the guys go, they'll beat us just like we beat them. We'll have to keep them subdued until we all starve or the next school year starts or something.

Then we hear a door slamming and feet running.

"Did you call someone?" I ask Sasha.

"No. If I were smarter I would have called the police..." Why did I think we could handle this?

"Yeah, same." I lean back to see down the hallway, and Luke takes the opportunity to break out of my arms and punch me straight in the face.

It feels like my eye exploded.

"Oh my God." I manage to pin Luke back against the wall, but I don't know how, because I can't think about anything but the burning on my cheekbone. I've seen people get punched in the face all the time on TV, and they never look like it hurts this much. God.

But as soon as I open my eye, I wonder if Luke hit me hard enough to knock me unconscious or something, because the two people running toward me are the top two that I would choose out of anyone in the whole world to help get me out of this mess.

The first is obviously Marco.

The second is Brian.

And he's holding Robbie. Top three.

Marco's legs are half the size of Brian's, but he's running like all of our lives depend on it. He runs into me so hard I almost fall over. "Did he hit you?"

I don't say anything, but I'm still holding my face like my nose is going to fall off.

Brian says, "Are you all right?"

Robbie whimpers my name. He looks really sick.

I say, "Hey, buddy . . . what are you guys doing here?"

"You hit him!" Marco screams at Luke.

Brian says, "Marco called me. Said you needed me.

I was driving around with Robbie…Christ, are you all right?"

"I'm fine…" I turn and look at Marco. Marco who called Brian. Who called someone because he thought I needed him. Who called my *brother*.

He's still screaming at Luke, spitting and cursing in English and Italian all at the same time, and then he cranks back his fist and aims it straight at Luke's jaw.

"Wait," I say.

Marco looks at me. "Wait," I say again. "Let me do it. Let me get this one for you."

Marco pauses. He's thinking about it.

Then Luke sneers, "Aw, *Stevey,* let him do it. How much damage can a limp wrist do anyway?"

I charge toward him, but Marco yells, "No, *this one's mine,*" and he punches Luke right in the face.

It's probably not the right thing to do.

But it feels so good. Almost as good as when, while Luke's still reeling, Robbie leans over and throws up on his shoes, and Marco rubs his back and cheers for my kid brother like he does for Benji when he wins a soccer game.

SIBLINGS

Brian makes this big show out of glaring at me and Marco for hitting Luke, but really I think he was hanging back long enough for us to do it. "All right." He pulls us all apart and tosses his cell phone to Sasha. "Call the third number on speed dial and tell him to send a cop over."

"O-okay," she says.

"Relax," I say. "Brian's a good guy."

"Not you," Marco says to the guys on the floor. "Don't you relax."

Luke stands there, wincing and watching us.

Brian hands Robbie to Marco so he can check my cheek. Robbie's crying, poor guy.

"How'd you get here so fast?" I ask Brian. "Traffic's stopped everywhere—God that *hurts*, don't press on it." I take Robbie from Marco. I figure bouncing him is a bad idea, so I rock back and forth with him a little instead. "Okay. It's okay."

Luke glares at me. But he can only look so intimidating with a bloody nose and my brother's puke on his shoes.

"I was in the area," Brian said. "You didn't break anything, I don't think." He pulls me in by my hair, kind of roughly, and kisses the top of my head. Sasha steps away with the phone and the boys get off the floor. They're dazed and bruised but okay, and they look at Luke and each other and then back to Luke.

"Should we run or something?" Chris says, finally.

Luke groans and rubs his cheekbone. "Shut up."

"Don't push on that eye," Brian says, and he goes to Luke and takes a look at his face. He's not even pretending to handle Luke's cheek as gently as he did mine, and Luke keeps wincing and groaning. But he doesn't pull away, and the other guys don't suggest running away again. Guys my age are always scared of Brian.

But he's a good guy.

"Mr. Brewin asked me to keep an eye on the place," Brian says. "Guess I didn't do a good enough job."

"Jessica's dad?"

"Head of the school board, yeah," Brain says. "Told me he suspected people would be breaking in tonight, asked me if I could do a drive around. And since Robbie started crying whenever the car was stopped..."

I say, "He's falling asleep now, I think." His head is on my shoulder. He feels so warm.

"Didn't break in," Luke grunts while Brian presses on his cheekbone. "Door's unlocked."

"Yeah, somehow I don't think that's going to keep you out of trouble. I want names, all of you. You're the school board's problem now."

Brian copies down their names and I catch Marco watching Brian with total admiration. "We need a legal pad," he whispers.

I look at him, and he looks at me, and then we realize at the same time that we have no idea how to actually talk to each other after all the stuff that we said and everything that happened and everything we didn't ever want to say out loud.

We look down, and I swallow.

Two cops come really quickly, and they seem bored and tired, and they go through the same process Brian did of checking everyone's injuries and copying down names. Brian talks to one of the cops and he gets on the phone with Mr. Brewin and pretty quickly they say that Sasha and Marco and Brian and Robbie and I can go. I hear him tell the cop that I have pictures of the incident.

I just did detective work for the police.

I wonder if I'm going to get paid for this.

"Come on." Brian puts one hand on the back of my head and the other on the back of Marco's. "Outside, you two. And Sasha."

The cop says, "So the vandalism's in the auditorium?"

"Oh." I stop. "You need to get Marco's portrait down. We…before people see it tomorrow."

Marco frowns. "What?"

"They'll take care of it, Marco," Brian says. "Let's go."

Marco considers this for a second, then he shakes his head and steps into the auditorium. I can't see the picture, but I can see Marco, very still, looking at it. And crossing his arms. And smiling a little.

He comes out and says, "Let's leave it."

"What?"

He shrugs. "Looks cooler this way. It was a really lame picture, you know?" And then he smiles big. "Might as well go out with a bang, right?"

I don't know what to say. I think I'm proud but I'm so tired and so confused about Marco that I honestly don't know.

Then Robbie starts crying a little, so I pay attention to him instead, and I follow Brian and Sasha outside. Marco trails behind. He's still grinning his face off.

Once the four of us are outside, Brian smacks the back of Marco's head. "You're lucky we're the side that called the cops, you know that? Even *jerkweasels* can press charges for assault, Marco."

"Stephen got to him first," Marco says. His smile somehow gets even bigger. "He already had Luke cornered and everything. And he's the one who wrote on his forehead." He grabs me and hugs me. "That was awesome."

I say, "So you called Brian? Why didn't you go to the prom?"

Marco shrugs a little.

Brian says. "He called and said you were in trouble and that Luke was about to break in."

"How did you know someone was . . ."

Marco looks at me like I'm an idiot. "Because you told me."

This is probably the part where I'm supposed to give Sasha credit, since she's the one who really solved this mystery after all. But I really don't feel like it right now.

"We were worried about you," I say.

"I wanted to go to the prom." He shrugs. "But it was stupid. It's so late now anyway."

"How's the headache?"

"Hideous." Marco looks at me like he's thinking really hard. Then he whispers, "Are we okay?"

I wish we could just assume we are and not have to talk about it, because this means I have to think about it.

"I don't know," I say.

He nods a little. I think Brian sees the look on his face, because he touches Marco's shoulder, then hugs Marco.

Marco's expression is nothing I've ever seen on him.

"Thanks for getting me here," Brian says. "You're a brave kid."

"I didn't do anything," Marco says. Oh my God, he's blushing. He better not be getting a crush on my brother.

"Yeah, okay," Brian says. He's laughing a little, but then he gets serious and holds Marco at arm's length. "I would have hit him myself if I had to."

Now Marco's really blushing. This is ridiculous.

Brian takes Robbie from me and fusses over him a little, then he says, "Come on, you guys," and nods toward the car. Marco grins and mumbles, "I'll give you two a minute," before he bounds after Brian.

Sasha kicks the ground a little.

"You really brought it tonight," I tell her.

She looks up. "Yeah?"

"Yeah. Couldn't have done it without you."

She runs her hand through her hair. The bun's totally gone now.

I know she's uncomfortable, and I want to say something to put her at ease, but honestly I don't know what to say. I can say we really will still be friends, and I think that's true, but I also don't think we're going to be the same kind of friends we were. Although I don't know what kind of friends we were, really, because we weren't friends who ever really spent any time on each other.

And I guess that's my fault, but I don't feel bad about it. I don't know if that's good or bad.

It's just how it feels right now.

"Are you coming with us?" I ask.

She shakes her head. "I called my mom. She said just to wait here with the cop. God, is she freaked out. Good way to start the summer!"

I force a laugh, and she forces one back.

"So I'll see you later," I say.

She nods. "Yeah. Later."

I go to the car and slide into the backseat beside Marco. It's kind of dumb that I don't sit in the front next to Brian, but now that I'm here, it seems too awkward to move up.

Marco has Robbie on his other side, and he's playing with Robbie's sock. Robbie is half asleep and half watching Marco like he's the most important thing in the world.

"Wait," Marco says. "Brian, why aren't you at prom?"

He shrugs while he drives out of the parking lot. "Kind of dumb to go alone."

That sucks.

He says, "It's so stupid, but I was kind of hoping that if I, you know, caught the criminals, Mr. Brewin would be so impressed that he'd run and tell Jessica how amazing I am, and she'd take me back."

"So call Mr. Brewin."

"I was about to," he says. "But I guess I stopped being delusional and figured out that one night of playing hero isn't going to change a relationship that's been going sour for a long time."

Marco and I try not to look at each other.

I clear my throat and say, "Are you sure?"

Brian says, "She'd been getting sick of me for a long time, unfortunately."

"So that's what you've been doing sneaking around all the time?" Marco says. "Reconnaissance work at school?"

"Not exactly."

I say, "So where have you been going?"

Brian stops at a light and doesn't talk for a while. All I hear is the click of his turn signal.

Eventually, he says, "I've been visiting Dad."

Marco looks at me quickly.

I shake my head a few times, then say, "Oh."

I want to ask how his apartment looks and if he smells the same and if he's with that lady and if he's happy and if Brian tells him that I hate him like I wish he would.

I guess.

I don't know.

I want to ask if he wants to come home and if Brian's laughed in his face and told him, "No way, we are better without you."

I want to know if we're better without him.

"You okay?" Marco says, softly.

"I need a minute."

"Okay."

Brian says, "Stephen, it's okay."

I don't think it's okay. I just need a minute.

I take out the notebook and start flipping through it.

The pages are covered with photos of all the cases Marco and I have solved. Mrs. Dover's missing dog. Julia's lost homework assignment. The vandalism at my Hebrew school. I'd forgotten about that one.

Brian says, "Stephen, no one's going to make you talk to him until you're ready. But when you are . . . he misses you. He asks about you all the time."

I turn to the back of the notebook to reread the character profile I wrote on Marco. Except instead of Marco's page, I land on a different one, right next to it. It's in his handwriting, and for a minute I'm too busy freaking out that he saw the page about him to even read what he wrote. No wonder he has such a big head, when he knows all he has to do is open this notebook and read a list of reasons why he's awesome. I'm such an idiot.

Then I see the heading on his page.

STEPHEN KATZ.

I don't think I've ever been that shocked to see my name somewhere.

· Five siblings: Robbie [presumably a nickname of
    Robert, but this has not been confirmed],

catherine, Sherri [likely a nickname of
something, updates as events warrant], Julia,
Brian—keeps telling me that family is good; I
want to believe him someday
- green eyes (I like them)
- lent me half of his gym uniform when I lost
  mine so we would both get half points off
  instead of me getting all points off
- likes to go camping
- sleeps until noon if you let him—I don't even get
  that
- spit on the first guy who ever called me queer

I don't remember that.

- (I'll never forget that)
- hugged me to pieces when we were waiting for
  the ambulance after I broke my ankle

That one I remember, but mostly just that I was scared
out of my mind.

- listens to me
- the thing is that I don't deserve this kid at all,
  really

Okay.

So this isn't a relationship that's been going sour for a long time.

This is just my ridiculous best friend.

Brian says, "Stephen, no one's pressuring you. Really. Wait until you're ready. It'll come."

I'm having a hard time being too upset right now, after that. I don't know.

I say, "It doesn't... have to be a big deal, right?"

"No. It really doesn't. God, you're a good kid."

Probably someday I will want to see Dad again. Maybe I'll even need to see Dad again. But right now I don't. Right now I'm doing okay without him. So there isn't really anything to be sad about.

I feel so peaceful, right in this second.

I have so many people, is the thing.

If I need one more, Brian will tell me where to find him.

But I have a lot of people.

We're all quiet for a while, I guess trying to digest it all. I don't think I've ever heard Marco be quiet for this long ever. And he's not even the one to break the silence. Brian dials his cell phone in the front seat and starts telling Mr. Brewin everything the police didn't. I notice he skims over the part where Marco clocked Luke in the face. Brothers are really good for some things. I'd point this out to Marco, but I get the feeling he's figured it out by the way he's still playing with Robbie's foot.

I guess he doesn't have to be ready for his sister yet, though.

It'll come.

All of a sudden Marco says, "Look. I don't judge you for being Jewish or anything like that. Hebrew school is just really boring, okay?"

I'm smiling even though I don't want to. "Okay. Well, so is your self-righteousness."

He doesn't say anything back, so I work up the courage to look at him. I'm expecting him to be pouting, but he's not. He's smiling, really small and secret.

Then, in a voice soft enough to match the smile, he goes, "Fair enough." Then he looks at me and grins for real.

Once Brian's off the phone, I call up, "Hey, Brian? Where are we going?" We just passed the turn for our house.

"To the prom, right? Don't you guys have a heist or something?"

Marco and I look at each other. I wonder if I look as funny as he does when we're this shocked.

My brother is officially the greatest.

But Marco goes, "No. Wait."

I say, "What?"

Marco rolls his eyes, and his face is back to normal because he's giving me that look like I'm the stupidest thing he's ever seen. He says, "We have a heist." And he yells a cross-street to Brian.

THE ANSWER

The bus, like Marco predicted, is still stalled on the side of the road. All the passengers are gone, and it's just the driver arguing with the mechanic.

"Ready?" Marco says, unlocking his door. "We fix the bus and ride it all the way to the prom. You and me. Total heroes. The bus is our damsel in distress."

I say, "I thought taking a bus to the prom was lame."

"Our *own private bus,* Stevey. It's just a huge limo."

Then my chest gets cold. "Uh-oh."

"What? You okay?"

"How are we going to get into the prom? We don't have the note."

"Where's the stationery? Brian will write us one now."

"Guys," Brian says.

Marco says, "Brian, shut up, you'll totally write it."

I say, "I don't have the stationery."

"What? Stevey!"

"We'd given up on the prom at that point! And there was a lot going on, okay?"

Marco groans, but then Brian sighs and reaches his arm into the glove box. He roots around and pulls out a pair of prom tickets.

I snatch them, and Marco goes, "Are you sure, man?"

"I'm not using them, am I? You guys go. Have fun."

I dive into the front seat and give Brian the biggest hug of my life. He's cracking up. "Okay, go," he says. "Don't strangle me, Stephen."

"Yeah."

"Go get 'em, Tiger."

As soon as I'm off Brian, Marco leans forward and hugs him, maybe even harder. I kiss sleeping Robbie's forehead before I jump out and Marco, after the world's quickest hesitation, does, too. Then Marco and I scamper out of the car before Brian can change his mind. Brian's not an idiot and obviously doesn't leave us here with nothing but a broken-down bus, but he drives a little farther away before he gets out and watches us so we can pretend.

Marco watches him driving to the end of the block. His arms are around himself like he's giving himself a hug. "Okay," he says.

"Okay what?"

"You were right."

"About what?"

He rolls his eyes and goes, "God, Stevey, don't make me grovel," then he runs over to the bus.

And then everything goes from feeling peaceful to feeling pretty much exactly the way it's supposed to again. I run after Marco.

By the time I get to the bus, Marco's already translating rapidly between the mechanic and the driver. It turns out, the problem's minor, but the equipment the mechanic brought isn't working so he still can't get underneath the bus to replace the broken axle.

As soon as he hears this, Marco rolls his eyes. "You guys are idiots." He takes off his jacket and hands it to me. "Hold this." Like he's afraid of it getting dirty. Like we're not gross and muddy enough already. His cuff even has some of my blood on it.

I say, "Wait, what are you doing?"

He says, "Hello. Look at me."

He's gross and muddy, like I said.

He goes, "I'm *little*." And then he's on his back and under the bus like it's nothing. He holds his hand out for the new axle.

"Hey, car genius Stephen," he calls. "Coach me through this."

To be honest, the mechanic is way more helpful than I am, but it feels good to be Marco's sidekick again.

Don't get me wrong. Capturing Luke without him was amazing. But when I look back on this later, I'm going to remember Marco punching Luke in the face. I'm going to remember him as the hero. Because I know I can be big when I want to be.

Because I am standing here watching my Marco beat the whole world and I am ridiculously happy.

(And I'm also kind a proud of an hour ago when I got to beat it a little bit, too. Nothing *has* to be simple. I mean, look at Marco.)

He fixes the axle in no time. He comes out from under the bus covered in grease and grit, and he's smiling. He turns to the bus driver and talks in Italian, then he shakes his hand and smiles at me. "He'll take us right to the country club. For free. Even though I don't have my student ID. Uuugh my wallet."

"That's almost too easy." I wave at Brian so he knows we can go.

"Yeah, you can say it's too easy next time you're the one under the bus, how about that?" He leaps on my back and makes me carry him onto the bus. I don't know what to do with this kid sometimes.

The bus ride really is too easy. The bus doesn't break down. Or run into anything. We don't get lost. Marco's trying to act cool, but I can tell he's waiting for the other shoe to drop, too.

Which it does. The second we skid into prom, we realize that a pair of tickets is not going to fool anyone into thinking we're high school seniors.

The chaperone looks at me and laughs in her throat. I guess this is Ms. Tannelbaum. "How did you two get these tickets, hmm?"

Marco says, "Please?"

I put my arm around Marco's shoulder. "See, my boyfriend and I—"

Marco ruins it by pulling away and laughing so hard he almost falls down. Great. Now I don't know what I'm going to do.

Then someone behind us goes, "Are you Brian Katz's brother?"

I turn around. There's a tall guy standing behind us, and his face is like someone squashed Jessica's face and smacked it onto his head. I've never seen someone who looked more like another person, ever. It's kind of incredible.

He says, "I just got off the phone with your brother. I heard what you two did tonight."

Oh God. Did Brian rat me out after all? This is such a bad night to be arrested. It's about the only bad thing that hasn't happened tonight. And really I think we only barely escaped that because Brian promised the policeman my photos or my firstborn or something.

I crane my head around him and start planning my escape route. He's going to go right, so I can dart left and sprint through the door... Marco can take him down and then run after...

Mr. Brewin says, "Dolores, these two are free to go in."

I guess I should have seen that coming. Every heist needs a good twist ending.

Marco grabs my elbow and squeezes.

Ms. Tannelbaum says, "Are you sure?"

"Yes. A young man I trust told me I owe these two a favor." Then he gives us the no-drinking-no-drugs lecture we've heard a billion times, but we don't really hear it. We're both staring at that passageway to get into the prom like it's going to disappear if we give it any chance.

So the second Mr. Brewin says, "Okay, you two, have fun," Marco grabs me by the wrist and runs so fast I think he's about to pull my arm out of its socket before I can catch up.

The first thing I notice when we walk in is that everyone is really tall and no one is really muddy. We should have at least stopped in the bathroom and cleaned up a little.

The first thing Marco notices, I bet, is that Benji's band isn't playing. Most people are milling around instead of dancing, and the music is some Top 40 thing mumbling out of the speakers.

"Oh God," Marco says. "They're not playing. They canceled or something."

"You're the worst detective ever." I point to the stage. "Their instruments are right there. That's Benji's guitar."

"Yes! That's Benji's guitar!" He says this like he just figured it out himself.

"So they're just on break."

Marco cranes his neck and finds a door at the side of the stage. "They must be in there."

"So go on. Or are you still set on doing it onstage? You're really muddy."

But Marco doesn't say anything. He doesn't move.

I say, "Come on. You're not about to tell me we did all of this for nothing."

He laughs, just for a second. And he still doesn't move.

I give him a gentle shove. "It's all you, kid. I'm right behind you."

He nods. "Right. Okay. Come on."

Marco leads me to the door and pushes down the handle. His hand is shaking.

Inside, the band is flopped around on a dirty couch and a few beat-up chairs, laughing at some story Benji's brother is telling. Benji looks up and smiles at us. "Hey! What are you doing here?" He bounds over to us, then frowns. "You blokes are filthy." He scrubs some dirt off Marco's cheek. I'm surprised Marco's still standing, with the touch and the *bloke* combined.

"We came to see you," Marco says.

Benji grins. "That's awesome."

"It was really hard to get here. We had pretty much the hardest night ever. And it was awesome." Marco looks at me. "It was the most awesome thing we've ever done."

I think maybe he's right.

"We're about to go back on," Benji says. "You better mean you're hanging around to listen."

"No, we are," Marco says. "We definitely are."

He grins. "Good."

"Hey, Benj, it's time," his brother says.

"Okay," Benji says, then he turns back to us. "I got to go. Stick around after the thing and we'll talk, okay?"

"Can we talk now?"

All the band members but Benji are onstage now, but Benji still says, "Of course."

Marco closes his eyes for a minute, then he opens them up, wide. "See, the thing is…"

Say it, Marco. Say it. You can do it.

"The thing is that I really like you." Marco rubs his forehead, hard. I'd forgotten all about the headache. "I like you so much that I'm not sure *like* is even the right word. I just…I think you're incredibly incredible, and I couldn't let you go back to England without telling you that. It's not that I'm expecting anything. I know that I'm…that I'm short and I'm loud and I know too much about Sherlock Holmes and not enough about soccer, but Sherlock Holmes was British, at least, so there's that, but I still know that there's really no chance you're going to like me back. So this isn't about that, really. I mean, if you want to say…"—he puts on this pretty amazing British accent—"*Marco, I'm terribly desperately in love with you, too,* then don't let me discourage you or anything, but I want

243

you to know that you don't have to worry about hurting my feelings or something, because this isn't about that. It's just about me wanting to let you know how amazing and special you are and that I've never liked liking anyone as much as I... as I love liking you."

Benji is staring at him.

Marco waits a beat, then whispers, "So yeah."

Benji opens his mouth but doesn't say anything. Eventually, he goes, "Marco, I—"

His brother grabs him by the shoulder. "Time to go."

Benji looks toward the stage, then back at Marco. "I've got to go," he says, and then he does.

Marco sinks into me. "Oh my God."

I don't know what to say. I'm trying not to freak out because I know it will make him freak out, but God. I feel like I just got punched again. I don't think I felt this bad when Sasha rejected me.

"You did great," I say.

"Can we just go?"

I know this is so selfish, but it's hard to believe that he could possibly be more disappointed than I am right now.

That was the worst twist-ending ever.

I really didn't think it was going to end this way. I guess I should have expected it, especially after what happened with Sasha. But I always knew that this was so much more important than Sasha. And I don't know if that's because Marco loves Benji and I only liked Sasha, or that Marco's a guy in love with a guy and that makes it *different*, but something makes me so sure that it's not allowed to end like this. That he can't walk out of here heartbroken. Not after everything we did to get here.

But he's looking at me, and I can tell by the way he's rubbing his temple that he noticed the headache again. And he's about to cry.

"Yeah," I say quickly. "Yeah, we can go." We turn around and leave the way we came, and I squeeze his shoulder while we wade through the people toward the door of the ballroom.

Onstage, the band finishes tuning their instruments. Then there's this pause, and someone mumbling, and I'm curious enough to turn around and see Benji guiding his brother away from the microphone and taking his place behind it instead.

"I think he's going to sing," I tell Marco.

Marco turns around. "He can't sing."

We're in the back of the ballroom, now, and I get up on a chair so I can see. "Come here," I say, and he scrambles up next to me.

Benji clears his throat and searches the audience. I see him see Marco.

He looks down for a minute, then up, and says, "This is for Marco." And he steps out of the spotlight to let his brother sing again. Because he can't sing. And this isn't a movie, I guess.

But Marco could not be smiling harder if the song were written for him.

I cup my hand around the back of his neck and just hold him there for a second.

This shouldn't be happening. The charming soccer star shouldn't leave threatening notes in anyone's locker, obviously, but he also shouldn't love my angsty best friend, and who knows if he really does, or if he just feels bad. Maybe the glances he gives Marco in between chords are only guilty ones. But I don't think they are. But, logically, they should be.

And we shouldn't have gotten to this ballroom. And maybe he shouldn't have hit Luke. And Marco shouldn't be standing up above every one of the seniors right now. And we shouldn't still be glued to each other when in three months we're going to separate schools and that's just a lot bigger than him. I shouldn't be standing next to Marco, watching him get every flurry of chords and every little glance that he's ever deserved, and feeling that the victory is as much mine as it is his. And we shouldn't even be friends anymore, probably.

But we are.

And I am.

And that soccer player, that ridiculous English boy, that incredible bass player, is stopping in the middle of the song while everyone plays around him, and he's looking up and mouthing, "Marco."

And I swear Marco mouths, "Polo."

And then my best friend, my ridiculous incredible best friend, is running up to the stage, and Benji is pulling him into the shadows on the edge of the stage while the band starts another song. And Benji is kissing him.

And Marco has one arm wrapped around Benji and the other out toward me, straight, ending with a thumbs-up. Marco, you're so stupid. Let this be about you and him. I'm fine here.

A pretty girl in a red dress looks up at me and says, "Hey, do you want to dance?"

And I am either laughing or crying or maybe a tiny bit of both.

And I dance.

ACKNOWLEDGMENTS

A million thank yous, as always, to my incredible editor Nancy Mercado and the entire team at Roaring Brook for helping me twist this little idea all the way into a book. Thank you so much to my lovely agents, Suzie Townsend and John Cusick, for their enthusiasm and support. I'm of course in endless crazy gratitude to my parents, my sister, my aunts and uncles and cousins and grandparents, to Seth, Emma, Alex, Galen, and Madeleine, to my Musers, to my fish, and everyone who kept telling me I could when I was absolutely sure that I couldn't. Looks like you were right.